Dragon in the Mirror: Into Canonsland

Penelope S. Hawtrey

DEDICATION

For my husband who encouraged me to write this story.

And to all my family, friends, and colleagues who helped me in this endeavor after they found out about this impossible dream, thank you. You know who you are.

INTRODUCTION

In the spring of 2016, I created a short story titled, "Dragon in the Mirror," that showed poverty as seen through the eyes of a seven-year-old girl, named, Jayden. Jayden's vulnerability seeps through in the first tale, but I didn't leave her alone with her fears and emotions. I added a small dose of fantasy when I included a connection between Jayden's companion, "Bob the Dog," and a dragon that she sees through her bedroom mirror. The dragon isn't alone, as well, and he comes with his own friend, protector, and companion, who's a knight—named Wyndham.

From there, a bond is formed between Jayden and the knight. Wyndham makes a promise one evening to a frustrated and hopeless Jayden that things will turn around for her family. When a stranger, William, arrives, he hardly seems like the type that can help Jayden's family. But, looks can be deceiving.

Nearly four years after the publication of "Dragon in the Mirror," on Amazon, this novel picks up with Jayden as an eleven-year-old girl who loves her home, parents, and Bob the Dog. However, Jayden's family now faces a more significant challenge than ever before, and secrets kept divide this one-time close-knit family.

Many of the same themes covered initially in the first short story can be found again in the novel. However, Jayden also grapples with many new and different problems by continuing to be the astute observer that we met in the first few pages of the introductory story. Her ability to observe, act, and empathize is one of the characteristics that makes her capable of handling new challenges she encounters in Canonsland.

After careful consideration, I've included in this book, the original short story as a prologue to the novel as many people who read the first draft felt it was necessary. So, this is your invitation to meet my friends: Jayden, Robert, Lisa, Wyndham, and the "Bobs," as well as many new characters.

Come with Jayden, as she faces new obstacles at home—and then dives into the beautiful and dangerous world of Canonsland.

PROLOGUE

"What does he look like?" Momma asks as her left eye twitches, and she fiddles with the brown strings dangling from her sweater. In the background of our kitchen, some song plays on our radio. We found the radio at a garage sale last summer because our other one *just stopped working for no good reason,* Daddy said.

Mom's sweater smells like cheese and macaroni from supper that we had two nights ago and coffee from this morning. Momma's worn that sweater every day for the last five days because our washer and dryer are busted, and she has no change to use the laundromat in town. She hand washes my clothes for school so that I don't smell. But Momma and Daddy have to do without. The washer broke a month ago and the dryer last week. Daddy said, *maybe next week, we can get them fixed.*

"He kind of looks like Bob," I say as my mouth turns upwards into a smile. Without meaning to, my brown eyes expand a little more than usual with hopefulness at Momma. I want to share with her what Wyndham told me last night. But as she stares down at me pale-faced, I shift my glance away from her. Momma doesn't like to hear about the dragon or the knight. I look down instead at my black-eyed pup that we named Bob. Bob smiles at me with bright eyes.

"Jayden, honey," Momma says.

I'm scared of what she will say next.

I stare down at the dirty black and white checkered floor. Crumbs and gravel stick to the bottoms of my socks. I lift my foot to shake them off. Momma sleeps a lot lately. She said to me yesterday: *I know I should clean the floors. But I'm so tired of trying to make things work with nothing.*

When I look up again, Momma has a thin smile on her lips. Her eyes are gray in color if that's possible—gray eyes that make me think someone stole her soul last night. Momma's skin is delicate; her lips are cracked from the cold, and bits of blood weave their way between the cracks like rivers on maps.

With a screech, Momma drags the peeling wooden chair out from the kitchen table that belonged to Grandma before she died a few years ago. She picks me up and sits me down on her lap. Behind her, the wallpaper is flaking on the kitchen wall.

Momma wraps her arms around me, and I play with the dead, dry skin on her hands. As she leans into me, I feel the warmth of her breath in contrast to the cold in our house. I heard Mom and Dad talking last night: Daddy couldn't pay the gas bill, so the company turned the heat off yesterday. Right now, Dad's at the company trying to convince them to turn it back on.

"Jayden, honey," Momma begins again. "I know it's hard for you. But you can't keep pretending that Bob becomes a dragon at night. You're seven years old now. *Imaginary friends are only for really small children. People in town are starting to talk.*"

I should never have told that girl at school, Allison,

that Bob turns into a dragon at night when he sees himself in my bedroom mirror. Bob the Dragon doesn't say much: Just sniffs and stares at me with big brown eyes. Sometimes the dragon will tilt his head like he's trying to figure me out, just like Bob the Dog does. But Bob the Dragon has a master that's a knight—Wyndham and I, we've talked.

"But Mom," I start to say as my eyes burn with tears, and my lower lip trembles.

I have to tell her.

"Momma, Wyndham says that he's coming to help us! You have to believe me!"

Momma shakes her head with the dried blood on her lips. She sighs at me, and as her eyebrows droop to each side, her face softens, and she says, "Honey, I would love it if there was a knight that was coming to help us. But baby," her chin drops, Momma shakes her head from right to left, and she cries, saying, "that's just not going to happen for us."

Momma's eyes won't look at mine, so I wrap my arms around her. I can feel Momma's heart pounding in her chest as she chokes and gasps through tears.

The door pushes open from behind us, and we both jolt out of our embrace. Momma uses the sleeves of her sweater to wipe her face, pushes me gently from her lap, and she says to Daddy, "Any luck?"

Daddy doesn't answer for a moment, and I realize that the same person that took Momma's soul last night— took Daddy's today.

Daddy's eyes are dim, and he stares at Momma as if I weren't there.

Momma turns to me, and then her thin smile is back, and she says, "Honey, can you go to your room? And take Bob with you."

As I start to climb the stairs with Bob circling me, there's a knock at our door. I watch as Daddy turns around, scowls at the sound for a moment, sighs heavily, and then swings it open.

Bob, who was in front of me, turns around and leaps from the third step, charging and barking at the stranger. I rush to intercept as I know Momma and Daddy are in short tempers on days like today. Momma said last night: *If only Daddy could find some work. But no one's fixing their houses now because lots of people have lost their jobs. They won't be fixing anything for awhile.*

I hear a familiar voice say as he pushes back the hood of his sweater, "Easy boy!" with a chuckle. Bob wags his tail while leaping and slobbering on the stranger.

Daddy says as he pulls Bob back, "Sorry about that. Ah, how can we help you?"

The man says, "No, it's okay, I love dogs! Sorry to interrupt you and your family. But, my battery in my car is dead, and I had to walk a few miles to get here. Is there any chance that you could give me a boost?"

Daddy stares at the man with his long brown hair, short beard, and soft blue eyes. For a moment, Daddy's eyes are hard as if to say: *No one helps me. Why Should I?*

But then he grabs his keys, jingles them in his right hand, and says, "Sure, no problem. I'll give you a lift."

***

"What happened?" Mom asks.

"I guess it's not just a dead battery." Sweatshirt man says as he holds his duffle bag over his right shoulder.

"Just bad luck," Dad says with a chuckle. "We know what that's like, eh, Lisa?"

Mom doesn't laugh but sighs heavily and says, "We sure do."

Mom turns and says, "Robert says your name is

William?"

"Yes, Ma'am," the man says. He pauses, looks around for a few seconds, and asks, "Ah, where should I put my bag?"

"You can put your bag in the living room. Small place, so we only have the couch for you to sleep on. Is Kraft macaroni and hot dogs for dinner, okay?"

"That's great," William answers.

Mom's eyes squint a bit as she stares at William. With her hands on her hips, she asks, "What happened to your cheek William? It looks like you got cut?"

"Oh, it was a tree branch! It just kind of slapped me in the face!" William says as he swings his head back in laughter.

"Let me get you some ointment to put on that. You wouldn't want it to get infected," Momma offers.

"No, thanks, Ma'am. I'll be fine." William answers as he waves his free hand at her as if to emphasize he *really will be fine.*

He turns to me and asks, "Who's this?"

Dad says, "Oh, this is our daughter, Jayden."

"Hi," I smile, bashfully.

"Hi Jayden, it's nice to meet you," William says as he swings my hand up and down, exaggerating our handshake.

***

At dinner, I announce to William, "This is our third meal this week of macaroni and cheese. Momma ran out of butter and milk a couple of days ago. So, this one's only made with the cheese from the box and water. It's a little soupier than normal."

For the first time all day, I watch as Momma and Daddy's face flush red with color at my announcement. Their eyes shift back and forth as they try not to look at

William. It occurs to me I just embarrassed them in telling William, the stranger, about the butter and milk. I glance down at my plate, avoiding Mom and Dad's eyes.

William says, "It's absolutely delicious. Best food I've had in days." As I look up at William, he gives me a secret wink, and I feel better.

William turns to Daddy and says, "I really appreciate your hospitality—the food and a place to sleep tonight. I feel bad about this, but can I ask you for one last favor? Would you mind driving me to town tomorrow so that I can arrange for a tow truck to pick up my car?"

Daddy's shoulders are hunched forward, and he says, "Certainly, of course." He says the words without even looking at William.

I watch as Daddy's shoulders roll forward a little more, and his chin drops. He looks smaller than ever before. My eyes turn away and focus on the wiggly cheese parts and two sticks on my plate. I don't dare look up in fear that Daddy will disappear in front of me.

From the corner of my eye, I see William glance for a few seconds at Momma and me. A few minutes later, he turns his attention to Daddy. He says, "Robert, I'm lucky to have met you. I haven't had a meal in a couple of days, and I've been sleeping in my car trying to make it across the country. I have a job lined up in Vancouver, and without your help tonight, I don't stand a chance of making it there. Most people would have turned me away."

I lift my head and watch as Daddy's shoulders roll back, chin lifts, and his eyes come to life. He smiles and says, "Happy to help where I can, William."

My head turns to Momma. But she is still shrinking away.

I focus on my food again.

***

From my parent's bedroom, I hear Dad say, "Lisa, did you get your baby bonus today?"

Mom says, "It's not called a baby bonus anymore, Robert. It was called that when we were kids. But yeah, I did. Why?"

"I don't have any money left for gas, and I'll barely have enough gas to get William to town. Can I have your bank card?"

"Robert, we were going to get the washer and dryer fixed with that money!" I hear Momma hiss at him in a whisper.

"I know. But even if I didn't drive William to town, I still wouldn't have any money left to look for work."

There's a pause.

I hear Momma sigh. Then she says, "You're right."

I hear Momma's slippers flip-flop across the floor as the wood creaks, and the walls shrink in around me, suffocating me in the darkness.

"Here's my card," Momma says.

***

"Jayden," I hear from behind me.

"Yes, Wyndham," I say as quietly as I can in hushed tones so that Momma, Daddy, or William don't hear me. I roll over to look at Wyndham through the mirror, and I see a cut on his cheek.

"What happened to you?" I ask in a louder whisper. "You have a cut on your face!"

"Wretched man in town beating a young lad for taking some bread: The child's family was starving. I offered to pay the scoundrel three times the cost, but he refused. Preferred, I suspect, for the boy to pay with lashes. I tried to restrain him without wielding my weapon, but the man drew his sword upon me. Bob, with one mighty blow of breath, knocked the rogue to his feet. Then I rode Bob as he carried that sobbing rat by his collar, high over London's green meadows to face his Lord.

"Wyndham, you have to be careful!" I shriek. "You're my only friend! I can't lose you!" I say as my throat fills with tears.

"Do not concern yourself, Jayden, with this wee scratch on my face. You have seen me far worse. What has happened that a small graze causes you such despair tonight?"

In muffled tears, I say, "Momma's disappearing. I almost lost Daddy tonight, but he came back. But Momma may still leave."

"Jayden, I promise you, one more day. Tomorrow will be better."

I take a deep breath in as Bob blows in my face. I wrap my arms around his black and white coat and hang on tight.

***

I wake to hear Daddy's red F-150 truck rumble out of our pot-holed stone driveway. I reach my bedroom window just in time to watch a combination of slushy brown snow and rocks spray up the sides of the truck and onto our lawn. I see two small heads in the cab of the truck get smaller as they drift along the road. Daddy's blinker signals that they will turn right and with that turn, and they are gone from sight.

My hands shake from the cold, teeth chatter together as I dig through my dirty clothes hamper to find my second pair of pajamas. *Momma told me to wear layers.* I pull another pair of socks over my toes—but the frigid wooden floor penetrates through to the skin on my feet. I patter out to the front hallway, and grab my dirty running shoes with the open lip on the front and lace them up to wear in the house.

Momma's sitting at the table, and as I pass, she asks, "Honey, do you want a couple of eggs?"

"Sure, mom," I say in a quiet voice.

Momma stands at the stove, and I hear the frying pan crackle, and then the smell of egg is everywhere.

"Mom, what are you using to cook the eggs if we ran out of butter?" I ask in a cautious whisper.

Turning around, Mom breaks into laughter, and says, "You're having scrambled eggs, baby. It's a non-stick pan so that the eggs won't stick. So, we don't need butter or milk, just water. And as long as I stand over them and push them around, they won't burn."

"Oh," I say and smile at Momma. I'm grateful for a few moments when she doesn't look sad.

"Honey, would you mind getting me my brown sweater? I left it in the living room."

"Sure," I reply. I'm happy to help Momma keep warm.

I was kneeling on my knees on the wooden chair at the table, so I swing my legs out, and my running shoes clunk against the floor.

When I enter the living room, I grab Mom's sweater that's stretched out across our sofa. Across from the couch is our well-used coffee table where a framed picture of Granny sits and against her photo is an envelope with these words written: *Robert, Lisa, Jayden, and Bob.* I grab the letter and bring it with Momma's sweater.

As I enter the kitchen, I say, "Mom, I found an envelope that's addressed to us. Did you see this?"

Mom's face scrunches as she looks carefully at the package. She says to me, "that's weird. It's not just paper inside the envelope. It feels like there's something else. We'll wait till your father gets back to open it."

***

When Daddy returns, we tell him about the envelope. He tears it open and reads to us:

Dear Robert, Lisa, Jayden, and Bob,

Once again, I can't thank you enough for your kindness and hospitality last night. I've always thought that it's easy to be generous when you have a lot, but when people have nothing, would those people help a stranger?

Well, I don't know about other people, but Robert—you and your family are exceptional. Over the course of last night, it became obvious to me that you have your own financial problems to worry about, but in spite of this, you drove me to my car, offered me what little food you had, gave me shelter for the evening, and were willing to drive me back to town today. As well, I watched as you fed Bob his dogfood, and somehow, that spoiled dog ended up with a few pieces of hotdog in his bowl as well!

As you probably gathered, I don't have much. But I do have a great job lined up in Vancouver that starts on Monday, and as I mentioned last night without you, I wouldn't have a chance of making it there on time. So, I made a decision.

Enclosed, you will find two coins: A gold five and ten dollar piece issued in 1914. Very few coins were issued and distributed that year because of the outbreak of the First World War, and this made the few coins issued more valuable because they were so rare. These two coins were willed to me by my grandfather. I have had them appraised at different times in my life. The last time I had them valued, the $5 coin was assessed at around $1,500, and the $10 piece was estimated to be worth about $2,000. Until last night, I was unable to part with them. But then I met you, Robert, and your extraordinary family.

These coins are a gift for your kindness. I recommend you take a trip tomorrow to the city and sell them there. And please, make sure that you get a good chunk of change for them. It's not much, but I hope it will be a little help. And if you ever thought no one

cared, remember—someone does.
    All the best,
    William

***

After he read the letter, Daddy drove back to town to return the coins to William. Daddy said we couldn't accept them because William had less than we did, and his grandpa gave them to him. He went to the tow truck company where he dropped William off, but the people there didn't remember him. Then, Dad drove back to the spot where William left his car.

No car. No William.

We had no choice in the matter. We took that trip to the city and bought butter and milk on the way home. The next day, Daddy paid the gas bill, and the heat came back on. A few days after that, the washer and dryer got fixed.

***

"Sweet child, how are you this night?" Wyndham asks.

"Happy," I say.

CHAPTER 1

Four Years Later

Last year me, mom, and dad were in our truck and weaved along the highway somewhere between Alberta and British Columbia. Out of the windows, carved rocks slid by on both sides of our vehicle. Then I saw a sign with a triangle on it with small dots that tumbled along one of the edges. I asked dad about it, and he said, *Jayden, it's a warning sign for falling rocks.*

A few minutes after I asked the question, a drizzle of small pebbles danced along the edge of the mountain and hit our car, and one of the larger rocks struck the glass of our windshield in just the right way and left a coin-sized hole in it. Dad was prudent and had the windshield fixed. He said *if we don't fix it, the small problem will get bigger.*

We didn't know it before, but the small stones that we faced earlier in our lives were nothing in comparison to the boulder that has now been hurtled towards us. Worse yet, this may be one of those situations that all attempts to fix it will still have the same final result: Our car will be destroyed.

My fists are balled at my side, and my teeth are locked

together. Bob stares up at me with a tilted head. His expressive brown eyes seem to beg me to tell him *what's the matter*. His tail is limp behind him. After a few moments, he slinks up the stairs with the understanding that he can't help me. There's no happy puppy here.

I'm ready for a fight. I scream, "I WON'T GO! YOU CAN'T MAKE ME!" Then I turn on my heels and run up the stairs with my feet hitting the floorboards heavily as if to emphasize my position. It's as if with each one of foot stomps is meant to punch through the floor that would anchor me in my home.

If I'm anchored, they can't make me leave.

When I enter my room, I throw the door open and use all the force I have in my eleven-year-old hands to thunder it closed behind me. The walls of my room shake and my eyes catch a glimpse of a framed picture that falls off the wall and hits the wooden floor. I hear the smashing and splintering of glass.

"Oh no," I say as I race over and turn the framed photo over.

When I turn the photo over, my face burns with heat, and then small droplets of rain flow from my eyes. My lower lip punches out as if to gather the rain and save it for another day. *It's all about conservation.* That's what Mrs. Whitemore says in Social Studies class.

Conservation means protecting the natural environment. We must conserve and take care of the things that matter to us.

The photo is a picture of me, Mom, and Dad that was taken overlooking Lake Okanagan on our trip last year. We couldn't go for long, but it was the one and only trip we'd taken as a family.

Over my shoulder, I hear a puffing from behind me; it's a gentle puff, like breath flowing through a nose. It sounds more like a purring sound.

"Leave me alone, Bob!" I blurt out.

When I turn to look around, I notice Bob's in his bed that's in the corner of my bedroom. His body is wedged close to the edge of the wall, and he stares at me from there. It's as if he wants to be as far away from me as he can. This causes the small sprinkle of teardrops that begin as a slow dribble from a tap to increase in pressure, and now it's as if someone has turned the faucet on all the way. My tummy drops a bit as I look over at terrified Pup that prefers to be against the cold wall instead of anywhere near me. I fold over with the amplified salty pressure of tears that stream down to my puckering lip.

The breathing wasn't Bob. Well, not that, Bob.

I glimpse into my bedroom mirror: *There he is.* My hands still clutch my treasured framed photo. Turning away from the mirror for a brief second, I assess the damaged item. My fingertips cling to it tightly as if I can magically fix it if I never let it go. Incredibly, even though the glass is smashed to pieces, the photo has not shifted in the frame. Satisfied that the picture remains in place, I crane my neck around to see the image in the mirror.

That's when I see a big, soft, brown eye that watches me as it flutters up and down whenever it blinks.

Bob is huge. I giggle at the eye as I forget for a few seconds about the fight I had with Mom and Dad downstairs.

There's nothing creepy about my friend Bob the Dragon's eye. It doesn't remind me of those ghost stories or movies where eyes peer through a framed picture and watch their victim. I know the person is the "victim" because the music playing in the background starts off quiet and slow and then gets a little louder as it grows more intense, screeching to a final conclusion. The music makes my heart race, and sweat gathers on my hands. I know there's perspiration on my hands because my fingertips slip together with all the moisture accumulated on them. It's also because just before something terrible happens in the movie, I throw my hands up to cover my eyes and slap myself in the face with my wet palms.

Those movies terrify me. When I told Wyndham about them, he said not to worry because he'll always protect me.

I continue to giggle and turn my head back to watch Bob the Dog. His tail thumps against the wall and begins a slow swish back and forth. Bob moves away from the wall and edges closer to the lip of his bed with his ears arched forward. He's waiting for an invitation from me: my voice carrying soft words that guarantee that now everything is alright.

I place the photo with the broken frame on my dresser and pick up the bigger pieces of glass off the floor and throw them in my trash can. I move to another area of my room where I'm sure there are no smaller pieces of fragmented glass and sit down.

Then I say, "Come here, Bob!" as my hands pat the bedroom floor, causing a gentle thumping sound. I'm lying to him, telling him that I'm okay when I'm not. But he doesn't seem to notice that it may not be the truth and prances happily into my arms. With a soft stroke of slobbering wetness from his prickly tongue, he licks my face as he's always done when he finally arrives. I wrap my arms around his neck while my hands stroke his velvety fur.

"Dear child, what has happened this night that you shook the foundation of thy house?"

In the time I've spent turning my attention to cleaning up my mess, and to Bob the Dog, the dragon has disappeared from the mirror. Wyndham stands in the mirror now, dressed in tights and a white linen shirt.

Good. I know he's not in battle right now because he's not wearing armor. I know he says I shouldn't worry—that he has no plans to leave me anytime soon—but he's always getting hurt. He's got sliced in the arm, stabbed in the chest, and cut on his face. Wyndham fights for the poor, injured, and weak, and he protects them—all of us. It's what he does. Wyndham has told me not to worry because Bob the Dragon takes care of him. But Wyndham still comes home with cuts and bruises.

Or worse.

Pup is as excited as ever to see Wyndham and the dragon. His lips are parted as he pants through his mouth, and this resembles a smile to me; ears are pressed forward in anticipation of some fantastic conversation that will happen, that may mean I will be happier for a little while than on the days I don't see them; his tail swings wildly from side to side, knocking a ball that was sitting on the floor across the room. I tilt my head and wonder if Pup feels the same way Bob the Dragon may feel about Wyndham: *helpless when he can't stop me from getting hurt.*

"Jayden, ten thousand nights pass as I wait for you to answer." His voice is crisp, crackly, and sharp like that of a man who has lived a long time and has answers. But at the same time, his voice is soft and flowing like fluffy white snowflakes that slowly drift to the ground. He sounds like a father who waits for an answer patiently, but not to provide one, *'tis forbidden!*

To myself only, I make fun of the way he talks: *What has happened this night that you shook the foundation of thy house?*

Couldn't he just say: *Jayden, why were you so angry that you slammed the door?* This brief detour in my thought process makes me smile.

"Jayden?" His voice is gentle and firm at the same

time. I've heard this before. Wyndham's indicating to me he's losing patience.

I want to lie to him, but I can't. I'm not very good at lying, never have been. My throat gurgles with liquid as I turn and say, "Mom and Dad want me to go away."

Wyndham takes a step backward from the mirror as if he's been pushed by some force. I can see through his beard that his face has straightened. There's no impatience with me written there anymore. He takes a step forward, as if he's reclaiming space, then smiles and says, "Come, now, child. You do not know what you speak. Surely, you are mistaken."

I turn my attention to Bob, running my hands through his fur. In my head, I shout, *MUST NOT CRY IN FRONT OF WYNDHAM!* A minute or so later, I turn to face him. I gulp back tears, and in a smooth, calm voice that surprises me, I say, "Mom and Dad want me to go stay with Grandma Imogene and Grandpa Sydney for the summer."

Wyndham places his hands on his hips, and his eyebrows turn lopsided in a quizzical manner. Then he shifts again, putting his right foot on a bench in his home. He leans in on his right elbow as his left-hand holds his right hand to steady himself. Wyndham says, "For certain, there is a reason."

Knock. Knock.

From behind my door, I hear: "Jayden, sweetheart. Could I talk to you?"

With the knock and the sound of Momma's voice, a wave of emotions run over me: anger, sadness, fear, and confusion. Wyndham stares at my face, intently. I watch his lips part as he takes a small breath in before he bows his head a little to the right. When he raises his eyes, and they meet mine again, he says, "Jayden, 'tis your mother.

Let her in."

CHAPTER 2

As I open the door, Momma comes into my room. Smiling, she says, "Hello, Wyndham."

"Hello, my lady."

I've told Wyndham that Mom and Dad are not descended from royal blood, and he shouldn't address them as *My Lord and Lady*. But Wyndham insists.

Wyndham said: *I have known those with royal blood who do not behave in a noble manner. Yet, your father and mother never falter. They have earned their titles.*

Wyndham told me that Mom can't hear or see him. But she pretends she can after William came that one time and gave us his grandfather's coins. William gave them to us so that we could sell them and pay some bills, buy food, and have the gas turned back on in the house.

Months after this happened, I asked Wyndham at one point if he was William. He said: *Child, how could I be in two places at once? Do you believe me to be the magician, Merlin? Do you remember: there was a man who had beaten a small starving boy for stealing some bread? That was the matter I tended to when William came.*

"How are you today?" Momma says, sweetly into the

mirror.

I can barely keep quiet because I know she's lying. But I don't want to upset Momma more than I already have. Instead, I just roll my eyes.

"I have food to eat, a home, a loving family, trusted good friends, a good and faithful dragon. All things have been provided for; in truth, I know I am very fortunate. Life is delicately and beautifully grand in this moment. How are you this day?"

Momma says, "I'm well. Thank you for asking."

It's another fib. I stand quietly beside her.

Wyndham has stepped back from the mirror, and his arms are relaxed by his sides. The lines on his face have also smoothed out. Wyndham's older than when I met him a few years ago, but right now, it's as if he's suddenly younger again. He says to Momma: "My lady, I do not mean to trespass in a place where I am not welcome. I must ask, though, as Jayden has mentioned it. Do you wish to send her away?"

With Wyndham's question, Momma's face flattens a bit. She's smiling still, but it's changed into a narrow thin line. She says: "Sorry, Wyndham. Could Jayden and I have a few minutes alone together?"

Wyndham bows forward, saying, "Of course, my lady." He turns, retreating into the darkness. I watch as he and the dragon disappear from view. The mirror now shows only me and Momma.

***

Momma noticed the broken frame almost immediately and cleaned up the smaller pieces before we talked. She was so worried about Pup getting a tiny sliver of glass in his paw. Then, she sat down on my bed and patted the space beside her.

The air was warm and dry in my bedroom. Outside my

21

window, there was a pink-red glow from the setting sun. With this last light, I watched branches and trees sway in the wind. I used all my strength to lift the window up and said to Mom, *I can't breathe in here. I'm just going to open a window.*

It was a good excuse because I was able to stick my head out the window for a few seconds and got the tears filling my eyes under control. I would save my tears for another day.

I slowly walked towards Mom and sat beside her, and twisted my fingers around on my lap like I do when I'm nervous. She placed her hands on top of mine to stop the fiddling, but she never looked at me directly. Her eyes glanced up at me for a few seconds before she turned away. I'm sure I saw that she was saving her tears as well. Momma said to me in a happy, pretend voice*: You're going to have such an adventure in British Columbia this summer! Horseback riding every day with Grandma and Grandpa, making fresh jam, and meeting new people! You'll see—you'll love it!*

I am warm, curled up in my bed, with sheets tightly wrapped around me, as only Momma knows how to do. Mom has just left now after giving me a good night kiss. I'm embarrassed to say that I cried a little. I wish everything didn't bug me so much.

From behind me, I hear: "Child, did you speak with thy mother?"

"Yes," I answer.

"What does she say?"

"I have to go. She says it's for the best."

It's been a few days since I overheard Mom and Dad talking in their bedroom. Momma was crying, but I've heard that before. But then a lower sob came through the wall that belonged to a man, and I knew it was Daddy who said in a gruff whisper of broken words: *Oh god-d, no-*

no, Li-Lisa!

Dad never cries.

After that, there was the higher and lower sounds of a woman and man crying that came uncontrolled and sometimes together, with the odd sound of sniffling.

In between all the sounds, I heard that word again, the same word that I had heard over and over when Grandma Nettie—Mom's Mom—got sick. Grandma died more than five years ago.

Cancer.

After that night, I've noticed a pattern: I have times when I cry and cry but never in front of Mom and Dad. During those moments, I can't stop myself, no matter what I do.

Then there are moments like this: When I've cried so much, it's as if I'm hollow inside. These are the times when I just sit without feeling anything, or if I'm standing, I stand limply, as if my bones have disappeared from inside me, and now all that's left is my skin, and it's only my sheer will that's keeping me from crashing to the ground into a puddle of mush.

I refuse to look at Wyndham. Sometimes Wyndham knows stuff that's happened to me without me telling him. I don't want to tell Wyndham the reason I have to leave.

"Well," I hear his voice crackle, "If you are to leave, 'tis time you came for a visit. What do you say?"

I bolt straight up out of bed, ripping the covers off in one toss. I've completely forgotten about not looking at Wyndham and hiding my secret. My feet hit the floor, and I charge towards the mirror with excitement, saying, "Really? Really, Wyndham?"

Wyndham has never asked me to come for a visit in the last four years, and because he didn't offer, I never thought it was possible. I'm running towards the mirror and don't turn the lights on. That's the reason I don't see my dirty jeans that I'd tossed on the floor a few days ago.

My right foot in one swift stroke gets tangled on the discarded pants, and I trip over them, crashing to the floor and hitting my head on the dresser with a *thump!*

In the mirror, Wyndham is bent forward in laughter. Then he takes a few steps backward, takes a few steps forward, and finally, he falls back, laughing louder at my tumble.

"Jayden, honey!" Momma arrives at my bedroom door and begins rattling the doorknob. I hear other footsteps right behind her voice. I know it's Dad.

I decide I'm not going to tell Mom and Dad about being invited to see Wyndham's world. I agree with Wyndham that Momma can't really see him and that she just plays along because she thinks she should. If I tell her, she'll worry that I'm running away.

I yell, "Sorry, Mom and Dad. I got up to get a drink of water on my dresser, and I tripped over my jeans that I'd left on the floor."

"Oh. Are you alright?" She asks with less panic in her voice but still with concern.

"Yes, Mom," I answer quickly. I want her to go away in case Wyndham changes his mind about me coming for a visit. I want to see Wyndham and Bob the Dragon for real—not through a mirror anymore!

A few moments later, I hear a creak against my door: "Jayden, you need to clean your room. Your mess is taking you down, one pant leg at a time!" From behind the door, Dad's gruff roar of laughter comes through.

I scowl at the door. *Dad always thinks he's so funny.*

Momma says, "Robert!" This is followed by what sounds like a small slap against his arm. (She always does that when he makes fun of me.)

Of course, she's not entirely on my side. I heard her snort with laughter before hitting him.

I turn to look at the mirror, and I don't see Wyndham right away. He's stumbling back and forth, bending forward, and then he can barely stand, moving in view and out of sight and staggering about just like Uncle John when he drank too much last Christmas. I scowl a second time, but this time it's at Wyndham.

Out of nowhere, I see a brown, white, and black tail swish from one side, and Wyndham comes briefly back into view as he is swept backward. He is tossed onto his red embroidered chair, and then it lifts with a final swoop of Bob's tail. I can no longer see Wyndham. Only his feet are sticking up from the chair as he sits upside down.

Wyndham is still laughing.

My face burns with anger as I whisper-shout in the direction of his feet and the upside-down chair, "That will teach you!"

"Thanks, Bob," I say to the dragon.

Bob's eye fills the mirror for only a second, and he gives me a wink-blink.

"What was that, Jayden?" Momma asks through my closed door.

I huff with impatience and say, "Nothing, Mom. I'll clean my room tomorrow."

"Okay, honey. Have a good sleep. Don't let the bedbugs bite."

Through the door, I hear Mom and Dad's bodies move away from it. Then a more distant voice says, "Jayden, I love you." Mom's voice is thick, and it sounds as if the words have been crushed together.

I choke on my words as water fills my throat. Somehow, I force them out and quietly say, "I love you, too, Mom."

"Yeah, yeah! We all love each other! Now back to bed! Remember, I'm the Lord of the Manor!" Daddy's voice bellows at Momma and me.

I roll my eyes. That's what I do now when I can't say anything, and my parents are being weird.

There's distant laughing, and then I hear, "Put me down, Bob!"

The voices get further away, and then I hear, "No, you're coming to bed, my Lady! Your Lord has spoken, and you must obey me!"

Dad can always be counted on to create chaos wherever he goes. *No squishy moments permitted.* (That's what he calls them.) It's who he is.

Wyndham is seated in his red cushioned chair that was upside down, but it's now upright. His right elbow rests against the armrest that he leans into as he uses his hand to hold up his face. Wyndham's fingers slowly run through his beard.

He looks as if he's putting a puzzle together.

I hate that look. Sometimes Wyndham has figured things out about me before I've told him. He's really good at understanding people based on their actions, how they walk, and how they say stuff. He once managed to figure out that I'd got hurt. (I was pushed off a swing by a boy.) Wyndham said he knew something had happened because I was limping when I came home, my tights were ripped (They were jeans; I've tried to tell Wyndham that's what they're called, but he can't seem to remember.) and my face was white.

He eventually made me tell him what had happened. Wyndham then told me I needed to tell Mom and Dad. He said, *Child, he is a boy and will make mistakes during his life. But, if his actions are not corrected, he will continue with his contemptible ways.*

After Wyndham said that, he continued to bug me about the "swing incident" for almost a week: early every morning and in the evening when we chatted. Wyndham wasn't really pushy when he asked me about it, but he asked me about it every time I saw him. And that week, I saw him A LOT!

While I liked seeing him and the dragon every day, I got tired of his nagging. I finally cracked and told Mom. She was furious. I asked her not to say anything to David's parents (that was the boy's name), but she did anyway. She told David's mother, and he was grounded for almost a week. I know because David played a lot of different sports and wasn't allowed to go. As well, both David and his mom came to our house, and she made David apologize to me.

When everyone heard what had happened to me, other girls told their parents he did it to them, too. (Apparently, David liked to see if he could push girls off the swing.) After that, well—

David is only allowed now to come to the park with his parents. As well, most days after school, he goes to practice for whatever sport he's playing, and then he helps his dad on their farm afterward. They don't give him a lot of free time anymore.

Wyndham was right, though. After David got punished, he's different now. Whenever there's a kid that's being bullied at school by someone else (which happens quite a bit), David is the first to defend them. *And he does it every time.*

But as for this puzzle, I don't want Wyndham to know. I just can't talk to him about it. I'm not sure how much of the conversation with me, Momma, and Daddy, that Wyndham saw.

I slowly walk towards the mirror. Once in front of it, I can't stand the silence anymore, and I say, "What?" My hands punch down at the exact time as I ask the question. I scowl at Wyndham in the mirror as the lines in his face smooth out.

Wyndham says, "Are you coming, child? I cannot wait a fortnight."

My mouth opens, and I can't say anything.

This is what I love about Wyndham. No matter how mean I am to him, he always forgives me. There's a sweeping sensation that washes over me as if I've been hit by a wave. My bedroom begins to spin as I stand in front of the mirror. Guilt is a terrible thing. I can't believe Wyndham still wants me to come for a visit.

I wonder if that's the reason Mom and Dad are sending me away. I really haven't behaved very well in the last couple of days. The door-slamming, picture-breaking incident was me at my absolute worst.

In a confusing way, my eyes swell with tears when I think about Momma, and there's a rock feeling in my tummy for the shrieking tone that I took with Wyndham, but I grin like it's Christmas Day at the chance to visit Wyndham and the dragon. I hope that if Wyndham sees my eyes, he'll think it's because I'm overjoyed to be invited to come and stay and not because of another reason.

I'm a little bit worried about asking the next question, but I ask anyway. "Can I bring Bob?"

Wyndham gives Bob the Dog a sideways glance and says, "Of course, I would not dream of inviting Jayden without her trusted companion." I can trace a small smile on his lips with these words.

I can't stop smiling as me and Bob make our way towards the mirror.

"How do we come?" I ask.

"Grab hold of Bob's collar and hold it tightly."

I do as I'm told and say, "Okay; now what?"

Wyndham jumps to his feet from the chair. With each one of his quick footsteps, his shoulders keep perfect time with his feet as he crosses the grey-stone floor. When Wyndham reaches the mirror, he stares at me through it. Then, he raises his black-gloved hand to the mirror, and I see it through the glass in front of me. Suddenly, a finger punctures the mirror, and before I know it, his outstretched palm is in front of me.

I can't move.

"Jayden?" Wyndham's words snap me back to where I am. "Child, are you coming? There is much to see!" His face is soft, and he's smiling. But he's also chuckling at me.

"Oh! What do I do?" I ask.

"Take my hand, child." Wyndham's voice is an echo-whisper. It's quieter and louder, all at once. It's a question and a lullaby. But the words are said with great importance as if Wyndham really does want me to come.

Still holding Bob's collar with one hand, I use my free hand to wrap it tightly around Wyndham's. Once this is done, Bob the Dragon, moves forward. The dragon's chocolate-colored eyes stare at me. I don't blink for fear that I will miss something. I watch as Bob the Dragon blows from his mouth dancing, white mist-crystals that circle our clasped hands. The ice crystals are cold, but warm at the same time. They are the same temperature as the warm, soft snow we get in wintertime when I can spend hours building a snowman or having a snowball fight with my friends, and don't even notice.

It's a comfortable cold.

Unwillingly, I blink.

I open my eyes. Pup stands beside me, and my fingers cling tightly to his collar.

"Jayden," I hear from above me, but a little to the right, a familiar voice that says, "You can now release Bob."

I glance upwards to where I heard the words spoken.

And there he is.

Finally, after so many years, I stand beside Wyndham and the dragon.

CHAPTER 3

As I walk around the place that Wyndham calls home, every part of the building is made of stone. It looks like a castle would as pictured to me in fairy tales, or in those far-off places across the ocean where remnants of thousand-year-old fortifications sit on rich emerald grass. From the mirror, Wyndham's home seemed to have big plush area rugs draped on walls and laid across the floor. Now that I am here and see the carpets up close, I notice the color is faded, and threads are hanging from it. There is a general mustiness in the air. My nose tickles, my eyes tingle, and then I explode with an "Achoo!!!"

As I look up, I see the dragon. Bob the Dragon, is different, too. Before, he looked exactly like my dog, but Bob the Dragon, is all white here. His eyes, though, are still a rich, deep brown. They are just like Pup's eyes.

"God Bless you, little one."

I wipe my nose and say, "Thanks. The dragon's different here." I blurt out to Wyndham.

"Yes," Wyndham answers.

"Why does he look different?"

Wyndham strolls to the other side of the dragon.

Bob's head is slightly raised, but his full body is stretched out across the stone floor. This makes it easy for Wyndham to reach him. Wyndham reaches up to Bob the Dragon and begins to gently rub Bob's head while saying, "Enisseny is a winter dragon. As his coat is white, he reflects that which is familiar to those people he chooses to reveal himself to. *But he will not take the form of anything.* Enisseny knows a person's mind, knows the things that they love. Many people are afraid of dragons. Enisseny has learned over the last thousand years that if he changes to something familiar to that which is loved, a person will not fear him. People are most comfortable with that which they know."

"Not everyone," I say stubbornly. *I want Wyndham to know that I'm different.* That he can show me things that aren't the same.

"Very well," he says, as he throws a glance in my direction and continues to rub Enisseny's nose.

"How do you know what Enisseny is thinking?" I ask.

"He will sometimes share with me his thoughts, although he chooses what he wishes me to see."

"Oh," I respond as if I understand.

I look up to the ceiling of Wyndham's home, and it's just high enough for Enisseny to fit into it.

Enisseny?

"Wait a second," I say, as I stretch my hands out on both sides. "You called the dragon Enisseny? That's his name?"

"Yes," Wyndham answers. He says it without so much as a micro-glance in my direction.

"Why didn't you tell me that was his name? You told me his name was Bob!" I say as my face scrunches together. I'm trying not to be angry with Wyndham, but he's lied to me already so many times.

"I never said such a thing, child. *You first called him Bob.* I simply did not correct you," Wyndham says with eyes that are fixed on me, forcing me to try to remember the day we first met.

"I don't remember that," I say swiftly, with a small hiccup in my voice.

I honestly don't remember our first meeting. But I'm sure I wouldn't have assumed the dragon's name was Bob, just because he had similar colors to my dog.

I'm sure of it.

"Perhaps it is I who am mistaken," Wyndham answers as he turns his gaze away from me and rubs Enisseny's ear.

Heat rises inside me, crosses my cheeks, and spreads out across to my nose and forehead. My eyes search for something else that's in the room to ask Wyndham about. But my mind goes blank. The quietness between us seems to last for hours, even though I know it hasn't been that long.

Was it me? Did I really name the dragon Bob, because his coat was similar to my dog's fur?

After a few moments, Wyndham stands up. I take a deep breath in, and I'm suddenly aware of a mixture of dampness that hangs in the air (of the castle?) that causes me to shiver for a moment. But, there is also warmth. The aroma of garlic, parsley, and pepper fills my nose and drifts along the hallways.

It smells like beef stew.

Wyndham takes long strides towards me and says, "Would you like some stew? My sister Constance is a fine cook."

In answer to Wyndham's question, my tummy ROARS! It occurs to me that we never had dinner.

With a smile, I confess and say, "Yeah! I think I'm

hungry!"

I smiled when I answered Wyndham, but my voice cracked. It's weird to me. It was in part because I remembered my earlier fight with Mom and Dad because we didn't have dinner, but also because I'd denied that I named the dragon Bob.

Wyndham says, "Come, Jayden, and Bob, this way!"

Bob, with his tail swinging, bounces along as close to Wyndham as possible. I watch as Wyndham pauses for a second and gently reaches out a hand and strokes Bob's head. Then, Wyndham stands up, and once in front of two large oak doors, he throws them open, revealing a group of about ten people.

Candlelight reveals a mix of women, men, and a child about my age seated at a large wooden dining room table. Red bowls with swirling green trees and flowers painted on them are set in front of each person. Above each dish, a wispy mist indicates it contains hot food. Cutlery is positioned to the side of each plate. Each person has a red glass in front of them that matches their bowls. There are several fireplaces. Over one of them, a big pot is hanging.

When they see us, all the people raise their glasses and say, "Welcome, Jayden!"

Wyndham half-raises his eyebrows in my direction, and I beam at him. My lips curl up at him as I gulp. I can't believe he's mentioned me to his family, and they know exactly who I am! I can't say anything. Stunned in silence, a smile is the only clue as to my emotions.

"Come, Jayden, sit here." A woman says to me while patting an open chair. Her blonde hair is rolled tightly into a bun. In spite of her best efforts, her hair is thick like mine, and curls escape and fall gently down her pale white cheeks. Her dress is dark blue and goes right to the floor, and her eyes are the same color as her dress. I'm instantly drawn to her warmth and kindness, and giddily continue to walk in the direction of the chair.

Halfway across the floor, I stop dead in my tracks. *I'm in my pajamas!* Wyndham arrives beside me, not a second later, and ties a black-and-red cape around me. He says, "Wear the cape for dinner. After, do you see little Petronilla at the end of the table?"

My eyes skip along the dining room table in the direction that Wyndham is pointing until they land on a girl about my size and height. With black, tightly curled hair, she enthusiastically flaps a small hand back and forth at me.

A giggle erupts out of me as I nod my head and answer, "Yes."

Wyndham bends forward and says, "After dinner, she will take you to where you will sleep this night. Tomorrow, she will find you clothes to wear in the morning."

My fingers tug at the velvety, soft cape as I adjust it. Wyndham takes me by the hand, and once beside the blonde woman, Wyndham uses his other hand and motions to her, saying, "This is my sister, Constance."

"Constance, this is the child, Jayden, I have spoken of who is much wiser and braver than her years."

"Yes, dear brother. You have said this many times." She says this casually, as she glances backward for only a second and quickly touches Wyndham's arm while she remains seated in the chair.

Facing me, with her soft sky-blue eyes, Constance says almost as a song, "'Tis good to finally meet you. Wyndham speaks very fondly of you."

Wyndham's standing at his full height. Proudly, he stares down at me. I inadvertently take a deep breath in, and when I exhale, it sounds like a tired huff.

I don't know what Wyndham's talking about. I'm not wise and brave. *I'm lost, alone, and scared.*

I would run away if I could.

I pause.

I guess I have.

My eyes flip back and forth to the kind-faced people gathered around the table. But if I ran away, this seems a good place to go. The home is not well maintained, just like my house, but it's filled with warmth by the people in it.

"Please, sit. I will fetch you some stew and bread," Constance says.

She pushes her chair back, and a screeching echo sound bounces off the walls. Her dress swings out from her, revealing black boots. She quickly glides towards the fireplace where a pot hangs above it. Constance reaches for a bowl from a nearby table and hurriedly scoops out stew from the pot, and then the steaming mist spreads from the cauldron to the dish. Next, she grabs some bread that sits on the table where the empty stacked bowls were kept. With one swift turn, her dress spins around her ankles, and she speeds back to the table with my food as if she's afraid of it cooling off before I get a chance to eat it.

I'm sandwiched in a seat between Wyndham and an empty chair belonging to Constance.

I watch Constance as she returns.

But behind her, I see a blur of something.

I crane my neck to see past Constance. My chest tightens, and my mouth opens in horror when I see two large black-brown-white paws rise up, and a familiar nose touches a bun. When he's within reach of the forbidden baked bread, his mouth firmly clasps it, and he bounces against the table, knocking it over before he speeds away.

I scream, "NO, BOB!"

CHAPTER 4

I screamed at Bob: *They're going to send us away, too!*

Petronilla tells me, "Jayden, 'tis okay. Do not worry. None are angry with you."

Bob is standing close to me. I sit on the bed's mattress with my legs swaying back and forth over the edge. Petronilla's bed is right across from mine, and she stares at me as she bites her lower lip. Bob's tail sways back and forth as he snuggles into my knees. Bob always forgives me when I yell at him.

But I know that people are different.

Petronilla bites and bites at her lower lip. It's as if she's trying to chew it off the way that Pup does when he gets an itch. Her biting grinds on my nerves until I can't stand it anymore. I explode at her, "Yes, they are! Everyone's mad at me!"

From behind Petronilla, I catch a glimpse of a man. *I know it's him.* But if I pretend I don't see him, then maybe I won't have to talk to him tonight. It would be great if he just hangs out there if he wants to and then decides to leave. Tomorrow, we can pretend that I never acted so terribly on my first night here.

Why can't I stop myself from being so angry? I blush as I gaze down at the stone floor. Bob. Petronilla. Mom. Dad. I'm so mad at everyone.

But most of all, I'm furious with myself and how I've behaved towards everyone. Bob leans into me and licks my hands while peering up at me with those big brown eyes. At this moment, I wish I had the superpower to miniaturize myself. That way, I could run across the floor undetected, sneak back into the mirror, and go home.

I would have to shrink Bob, too. But once we were home, how would I make us big again?

"Petronilla, I must speak with Jayden."

Shoot! No such luck in not talking to Wyndham tonight.

Petronilla stares at him with her dark brown eyes. Her face is white as if she's afraid on my behalf. Or maybe she's worried that she was wrong about what she'd just said—that no one was mad at me for my outburst at Pup. And now Wyndham probably also heard me blow up at Petronilla, too.

"Yes, Uncle," she says as she tiptoes towards him. Before leaving the room, Petronilla faces me for a second and gives me a half-smile. Then she passes Wyndham in the doorway and leaves us alone.

Her smile was the saddest attempt I've ever seen to try to convince me that it will be okay.

"Jayden," Wyndham begins as he walks towards me. He effortlessly grabs a wooden chair leaning against a corner wall, places it down on the floor, and sits across from me. "I did not bring you here only to eat stew and bread. There is a reason your parents are sending you away. Tell me. And perhaps we can find a way to convince them of a different course."

My lower lip instantly droops. With my head lowered, I sob, and stutter, "You-you-you c-c-can't-t-t hel-p-p,"

39

and then I wipe my nose with my pajama sleeve.

Wyndham grabs my hand, leans in, and says, "Child, there is no problem that I have not encountered in my over two hundred years of life. Do not think you are alone. I may understand what you now face and may offer some guidance with my experience through a rocky, uphill road. But if you do not tell me, I cannot help."

I've stopped crying and stare stupidly at Wyndham.

"You're over two hundred years old?" I ask with a small shriek at the end.

"Give or take some years. I do not celebrate birthdays as of late. As such, I have stopped counting, and I have forgotten what age I last marked. As well, time moves differently here. I would be much older in your world."

"Your brothers and sisters, are they that old, too?" I am shocked and surprised. For a brief moment, I think, *if Momma comes, maybe* ….

Wyndham holds my hand tightly as if he's trying to bridge a gap between us. His hands are coarse and dry, and there are several scars painted across his skin. Some old wounds are thicker and may have been deeper cuts. Other lines are smaller and look like extra lifelines.

That seems even more appropriate now that I know his age.

With the candlelight, his beard and his face appear darker. He's also more somber than I've ever seen him before. Wyndham seems to be stuck on something as if he's hit a pause button. He gently swings his head to the side and drops his chin a little before he says, "No, I have only known them for some fifteen years."

"You see, Jayden, when they were wee children, they became orphans when an illness swept through Rumbling Town. They were the only ones that lost both parents due to the plague, and there were no other relations. When their parents died, I knew as a knight, I could not care for them myself. I desperately searched the village for some other couple or family who could care for them. I found a few couples, but they were willing to take only one or two children. *They would be separated.* When I told them the news, the children wept. Unable to watch the children cry and be apart, I did my best to care for them myself. When the people of the village saw this, they rallied around and helped me when duty called me away, and I was forced to tend to other matters. The children that I raised were, in truth, raised by the entire town. But as the children aged, it seemed best to call them my brothers and sisters. As you can see, they sometimes care for me now. We are more or less equals."

"Oh," I say as my head drops down. I stare at the floor and watch a fuzzy spider cross it and wonder if it carries some poisonous venom. I lift my legs a little as it passes by my toes.

I unconsciously start swinging my legs back and forth. This causes a small breeze. With my self-propelled wind and the dampness and cold of the castle, it causes the hair on my legs and arms to stand up straight.

So much for bringing Momma here.

My head pops up. I have to ask another question. "How come you've lived so long?"

"I am bound to Enisseny, and he extends my life. Although, if I am mortally wounded in battle, Enisseny, cannot stop me from dying." Wyndham gives me a lopsided smile as he adds, "I must still tread carefully with my life."

I laugh at what Wyndham said. We are both smiling now, and we both know the reason why. *Wyndham is sort of careful. But, not really!*

Wyndham's long life is because of Enisseny. I wonder if

Momma were bound to Enisseny if she would live. But I know Mom can't do what Wyndham does.

I can see it now: my delicate mother with her fragile skin that, when it's too cold in the winter, will crack and bleed, somehow lifting and wielding a sword and fighting people that would rob peasant farmers who toil so hard to produce their crops!

I snort a little with laughter at this thought. Even if Enisseny were the answer to Momma's problem, I would never betray Wyndham like that.

Toil, where did that word come from? Ugh! Wyndham! He's going to make me start talking like him!

I snort again.

"Child, why do you laugh?"

My cheeks flame. The middle part of my nose between my eyes becomes increasingly warm. It always does that when I'm embarrassed. But I can't tell Wyndham what I was thinking, so I say, "No reason."

"I bid you good night, Jayden. Sleep well. I will see you in the morning." With that, he squeezes my hand just once, stands, picks up the chair, and places it against the wall again.

As Wyndham walks towards the door, I say, "I didn't tell you anything. And you asked me, too."

"Do you think I am so old, I have forgotten?" He turns to face me while saying this, grins and places his hands on his hips. "In time you may, or may not. But I sense you do not wish to tell me this night." One of his eyebrows is up, and the other is down as if he's challenging me to say that he's wrong.

A small sigh of relief flows out of me. *Wyndham's not going to make me tell him.* My lips turn upwards at him when he strolls towards the door and disappears through it.

A few moments after Wyndham has left the room,

Petronilla comes skipping back in and giddily says, "You see! I told you no one would be angry with you!" Her nose and chin are both raised a bit as she says this.

It's a clear sign that she likes the fact that she was right, and I was wrong. Usually, people like that bug me, but not her, and not right now. Instead, I nod my head up and down in agreement.

From behind Petronilla, Wyndham's head bounces back in the doorway, and he bellows, "Aye! Not angry with Jayden. My wrath is reserved for a child who listens at the door to a conversation that was meant to be private!"

Petronilla has her back towards the door. When she hears Wyndham's voice, she leaps a foot in the air, and I do the same!

Then she turns to face him. Her mouth twists to the side as if she's not sure whether Wyndham's serious or not. And, honestly, I can't read him either. Wyndham is really good at looking serious, even if he's not. It's a game with him. I've been the victim of it many times.

Wyndham gives Petronilla a toothy smile. He says, "Now, get thee to bed!" in a growl of a voice as if he's angry with us. But his smile and the way he laughs at us shows that it's all in good fun.

Petronilla erupts in high-pitched squeals, turns towards me, and we both throw our hands up in the air pretending to be afraid of Wyndham. We hurtle ourselves into our assigned beds, and the headboard to my bed smacks against the wall. Once in, we both yank the covers up to our chins.

The fire in the fireplace crackles. In the corners of the room where candles are burning, Wyndham circles and blows each one out.

When he's done, he pulls the door closed and says,

"Good night."

CHAPTER 5

As I was riding a horse called Lyra, I asked Wyndham why we couldn't take Enisseny. He said, *if you wish to see a blur of colors high above our world, then Enisseny is the best way. But if you wish to breathe in the sounds and smells of this world, to really feel the heartbeat of our land, riding horseback will give you the richest of memories.*

Wyndham was holding the reins of Lyra while expertly riding his own horse. I told Wyndham I had ridden once at Grandma and Grandpa's farm. Wyndham replied: *One time is not enough to make a person masterful in such a task.*

At that moment, I finally asked the question that had bothered me since I arrived and said: *Where am I?*

Wyndham answered while looking in all directions and said: *This is a place that is far beyond your stars and your universe. It exists in a yet uncharted realm of space on Earth. It will be found. One day. The name of our world is Canonsland.*

So, **NOT** London, like Wyndham, told me years ago. I sighed but didn't say anything to him.

In the air, there was a mixture of peppered honey, citrus, and sumptuous bouquets of roses. I understood why Wyndham preferred to show me Canonsland this way. If we flew on Enisseny, I wouldn't smell those scents or see the colors as vividly as I was doing right now as our horses sauntered along the green meadows.

Lyra and Buckley were keeping stride together for the most part. Every now and then, though, Buckley would try to pick up speed. Wyndham, in a relaxed whisper of a voice, would say a few words, and Buckley would immediately slow down again. Wyndham joked: *There is a reason he is named BUCK-ley.*

The view around us was incredible. At home, when I looked at evergreen trees, I saw only evergreens together. Here, in Canonsland, I saw a mixture of trees, some larger and some smaller, and they all lived together. Pine trees grew beside weeping willows. As well, there was also another difference in the color of the weeping willows: The color of the droopy leaves that dangled down was blue!

If the view around me wasn't enough, Wyndham began to recount stories about the dragon:

Canonsland is a vast and diverse area where there is snow and ice in the boreal regions, and yet in other places, there are sweeping lush green meadows that stretch out across the landscape as we see before us now. In the boreal where the ice and snow exist, there is a place, Winter Dragon's Lake that was Enisseny's home, or was, before he came to live in Rumbling Town.

Wyndham explained to me the lake was made of a solid sheet of ice. Even though everyone knew you couldn't break it, kids still tried because they saw Enisseny pass through it sometimes. The children were curious as to what was on the other side.

Wyndham said: *The children were never successful. Many children returned home with at least one broken bone in their feet and sometimes many. It was futile to attempt to break the ice. Enisseny is the only one who may pass through it.*

Wyndham described how Enisseny, a long time ago, lived in Winter Dragon's Lake alone and hid from people. The reason, as Wyndham said was: *Stories were told of a white dragon that, if caught, would give its captor eternal life. Lords, peasants, and even children would hunt Enisseny. To this day, Enisseny carries the burns, cuts, and abrasions left by shackles that they used to try to imprison him. The wounds are etched deeply into his skin. Once they captured the dragon, the captors would become reckless with their lives, believing themselves to be invincible. All of them found out too late that they were not given immortality. Nonetheless, our Winter Dragon did not trust those he shared Canonsland with.*

The people believed the stories told to them as children were real. Aye, there were elements of truth to the fable—some parts true, some sections enriched, other parts fabricated—while other important details were forgotten entirely. The most crucial piece that was forgotten: that it was up to Enisseny to decide if a person was worthy of eternal life.

Not all people in Canonsland hunted Enisseny. Those who resided in Rumbling Town were different. They formed a league of men and women who worked to protect the dragon. They were not warriors, though, and therefore when Enisseny would be captured, the league would ride with haste and report the circumstances to the King's Knights. I, was already, a knight as well.

At that time, Canonsland was in a constant state of shifting borders, and unrest spread across the land. We did not always come as quickly as we might have in more peaceful times. Many times those who had captured Enisseny would die within a few days. When this finally happened, as it always did, the people of Rumbling Town would release Enisseny on their own. After some years passed, they stopped informing us when Enisseny had been captured. They would just wait for the captor's life to end and release the dragon on their own.

The people of Rumbling Town had great affection for the white dragon. Not because they valued eternal life. For they could see the future: If you lived a long time, you would face losing all those around you that you loved. No, they did not want that.

To capture an animal because you wished to claim something from it seemed cruel to the villagers. Over time, Enisseny became well acquainted with the citizens of Rumbling Town because they always released him and never harmed him. From there, a friendship was forged between The Winter Dragon and the people.

Some years later, The Hunters, who lived east of Canonsland, destroyed their land's soil when they farmed it to excess, never giving the earth the care and time to heal itself. Unable to produce even grass for their livestock, The Hunters watched as their grayners (that resemble cows but stand taller), pigs, and chenchicks (large ostrich-like animals) died, too.

After this, The Hunters began to hunt close to their own homes. However, just as they overused the land and did not care for it the way they should have, The Hunters killed every wildfowl that flew above them, every land-based animal that walked among them, and every fish that swam in the Red Sea. With nothing left to eat, The Hunters left in search of a new home, and after many years spent wandering Canonsland, they came upon Rumbling Town.

A few other brave knights and myself, found ourselves by accident in the middle of the battle. We had journeyed to Rumbling Town the day before to tend to some tasks requested by the King and had come only to sleep for the night at the town. Under a red sunrise, we heard the screams of the people when the straw used to keep the rain out of their homes was set ablaze. That night, as the people fled from the heat and scorching fire, the most brutal of The Hunters were slaying the unarmed townspeople in the streets.

Prepared or not, we were knights and could not leave Rumbling Town for certain destruction. We watched in awe as some citizens, armed with pitchforks as their weapons, tried most bravely to defend their families and homes on that day. The townspeople fought alongside myself and about twenty other knights.

I lost many good friends that morn'n. Despite our most valiant efforts, we were outnumbered and ill-equipped to fight so many warriors. Then we saw above us white wings flapping long before we could make out that which was approaching us. As the clouds were clearing, Enisseny sailed from the heavens towards us. He screeched in such a deafening way, it alone could have halted a man in his steps. If that were not enough to stop The Hunters, the beating of his wings sounded like deadly drums. If neither the screeching sound of his scream nor the beating drums of his wings scattered The Hunters, he would blow ice-cold air on them and freeze the warriors in their place.

The battle turned for us in a moment, and then Enisseny slowly released each of the entombed soldiers one by one. Those that continued to fight, we ended there. Those that chose to leave were released and scattered like seeds in the wind. Most of them chose to leave.

There was one Hunter, though, that did not speak the truth when asked what he wished to do. He said he would leave. But as he passed by me, he turned his sword to Enisseny and attempted to drive it into the heart of our beautiful white dragon. I intervened, and the sword went through me. Enisseny used his breath to freeze the bleeding, and the doctor in town tended to my wound. I did not realize until some years later, as my friends aged and I had stopped, that I was given a longer life. The day I was stabbed by the Hunter warrior was the day Enisseny, and I, were bound together.

***

Wyndham told me this story quite a few days ago. It was strange then when we returned from our ride that day, and a Hunter named Osgoode was waiting for us. I was told by Constance that Osgoode had carried a white flag into the village and told them he needed to speak with Wyndham alone.

Before he left, Wyndham said that The Hunters were divided among themselves. After close to two hundred years of wandering Canonsland, they had returned to their own homes and found the soil alive again. Some of The Hunters wished to continue to wage war against other towns and villages; others wanted to live peacefully and farm their newly-restored land. The divisions within the group led to bloodshed among The Hunters. The dispute did not grow into a war, but there were rising tempers among the people. Osgoode asked if Wyndham would come to help end the battling and find a way for all The Hunters to live together again.

Wyndham left with Osgoode, and I haven't seen him since that first day. My long-time friend and knight tried to get me to go home right then, but I wouldn't do it. I asked Wyndham why he would go with Osgoode. After all, he had just told me the story about The Hunters.

Wyndham said: *I have told you a small part of the history of The Hunters. But this is a small part, and there is much more to their history. Do not judge them based on that alone. Every person, whether they are a Hunter or a resident of Rumbling Town, is capable of both good and evil. Remember that.*

I crinkled my nose at him. The sun was shining that day. It blinded me as I looked up at him as he was sitting on his horse. I guess it made sense.

But, I wanted him to stay.

Then he laughed the way he does, smiled at me, spun around once on Buckley, waved and said: *Do not fret, child. I will be back in a few short days. You will see.*

That was the last thing he said to me. It's been almost a week.

Wyndham is missing.

CHAPTER 6

"We have to do something!" I scream at Alwyn. Alwyn is Constance's brother.

These people. They really are a peaceful bunch. I can't get them to raise the alarm about Wyndham.

Enisseny was left behind, just like me and Bob. He's spent the last few days spinning around in circles, trying to get out of the castle, but he's unwilling to break through the wall or the door. I know he can do it. Wyndham's family isn't holding Enisseny back, but they're also not opening the front door for him either. I can't believe how polite Enisseny is about this.

It's frustrating. *Just push your way out, already!*

He must know there's something wrong. If Wyndham and Enisseny are bound together, maybe he knows if Wyndham's hurt.

Alwyn shovels hay around the horse's stall. He doesn't say much, this guy; he just does his work. Alwyn is Petronilla's father, and he's married to Idonea.

Eustace raises his eyebrows at me as if he's saying, quiet. He told me that he would talk to Alwyn. Eustace said: *Push too hard with Alwyn, and my brother will bury his heels in. Speak softly with him and gently nudge him in a different direction, and he may agree.* Eustace is going to try to convince Alwyn that we should start searching for Wyndham.

Eustace's arms are folded together in front of him. He gently leans back against the wooden door of Lyra's stall. In a quiet voice, Eustace says, "'Tis odd that Wyndham has not returned. There is a chance he may need our help. What do you say, brother?"

Alwyn continues with his chore. Then, after a short pause, I think I hear him huff before he says, "I say, no, brother!" He shouts in Eustace's direction for a second before tossing more hay haphazardly in the stall. A short time later and in a calmer voice, he says, "Wyndham knows best. He did not take Enisseny with him for a good reason. You, too, heard the rumors when we traveled to buy seed at Wringing Sound Station. Lord Fulke WANTS the dragon." Alwyn's face elongates with the word, *WANTS*. Wrinkles appear on his temples and around his eyes, adding years to him in an instant.

I know that I'm a kid, and I probably shouldn't ask questions, but I don't care. I say, "What do you mean, Lord Fulke wants the dragon?"

Alwyn continues to ignore me. *This guy. He probably thinks children should be seen and not heard.* My face turns red. I scowl while waiting for an answer.

Eustace says, "There are rumors the Lord wants the dragon."

"Doesn't he know the story?" I ask, as my lips punch out, and my eyebrows scrunch together with confusion. "The story, that the dragon must decide who gets a long life? Besides, Enisseny has already given it to Wyndham! I doubt the dragon can give it to two people!" I screech like a hawk with the last sentence. I take a step backward. I'm surprised by how loud I was. I didn't mean to sound like that.

Eustace's arms are folded over his chest. Then he releases them and steps forward. His eyes focus on the ground in front of him before he raises his eyes to me again. It's as if he's considering something … as if he's trying to decide whether he should tell me something.

I'm so angry right now. But I'm trying to hold it back. If I were a dragon, I would be breathing fire at both of them. They're lucky! *Just spit it out already!*

"Lord Fulke wants the dragon for another purpose."

"She need not know!" Alwyn shouts and slams his pitchfork through some hay, tossing it aside. Inside the paddock that he's cleaning, I watch the dried grass hit the wall and then pile into a corner.

Grandpa Sydney would not be impressed with his stall-cleaning skills.

I ignore Alwyn and ask Eustace, "What other purpose?"

"The dragon …"

"Quiet! You share too much, little brother! You speak as tale-tellers do at our King's court!"

I'm not done with this conversation. But behind me, I hear something. The doors to the castle given to Wyndham by Lord Everard when he decided he would take care of Alwyn, Eustace, Constance, and Laurence, swings open with a *thud!*

"No!" Alwyn screams. He's the first to sprint out of the barn. Eustace trails closely behind him, and I'm in last place.

That's at least how it starts off. Eventually, my arms swing wildly by my side, and my long hair is extended by the wind as I run towards the castle. My lower legs are on fire from the effort of sprinting, and I gulp in large amounts of air. I get light-headed from the running, and it's as if my heart is way behind the rest of my body. But when I see Enisseny standing outside the doors with Laurence on his back, I don't slow down but speed up instead, passing Eustace and then Alwyn.

I will not be left behind again!

I'm ahead of both of them now. If we were running a race, Bob would be first, and I would be second.

From behind me, I hear muffled sounds of huffing from Alwyn. Then he screams, "NO!!!!!" in a desperate voice. I know Alwyn doesn't want the dragon to leave now because Lord Fulke's after him. But Enisseny's free, and as he's the same size as a woolly mammoth, I doubt anyone can stop him.

There's wind all around me. Suddenly, I sense more of a breeze around my shoulder, and this causes me to turn around. As I turn, I notice Alwyn's hand is stretched out towards me, and he lunges for my elbow.

Alwyn's reaching for me! With my increased fear of being stopped if Alwyn catches me, I kick my speed up into hyperdrive.

Enisseny sees me. I watch as he stretches out his wings and hops on his talons for a couple of steps. This makes the ground shake underneath my feet. I lose my balance a little bit, and I unintentionally slow down. My lower lip trembles as Enisseny sails upwards and soars above the meadows.

Alwyn and Eustace are quite a ways away from me, and they've stopped, too. I stand there, waving my arms with my heart pounding, and scream, "Enisseny!"

As always, Bob stands beside me. Large tears fall down my cheeks. I lower my head. Suddenly, a gust of wind picks up, causing my dress to swirl around me. The grass leans quickly to the right and then to the left. The breeze makes me colder for a few seconds, and I cover my arms with my hands to keep myself warm. The wind sends my hair spinning in all directions, and that's the reason I see it—but I don't believe my eyes.

Enisseny's talons clasp around me and Bob, lifting us into the air as we take off in flight. With his four claws scooping us up, we are resting inside of what can best be described as the palm of Enisseny's hand.

I squeal a "YES!" to no one. I'm delighted because Enisseny is so smart—he must think it's important that me and Bob come along!

Wedged between his talons, we have a view of the world below us. Bob shifts from side to side, peering down for only a nanosecond before he backs up inside the dragon's palm. He begins to whimper softly. I stroke his fur and whisper to him, "It's okay, Bob. Enisseny won't drop us."

Bob looks at me with those big brown eyes, and his eyebrows twitch up and down every few seconds. There's something in his expression that implies he doesn't believe me.

As I peep out from between the talons, my tummy gets queasy. My happiness disappears, and now I'm consumed with fear. I lurch from side to side in the palm of the dragon. I sense the blood has drained from my face. My hair bustles around me. I grab clumps of it and try to hold it back, but it's no use.

No, wonder, Bob doesn't believe me. I suspect I don't look like I'm enjoying this either.

I stick my head out a little bit more, but this time I gaze upwards to see Laurence. I assume he's hanging on to Enisseny and is riding him on his back without a saddle. I don't recall seeing one.

My grandfather and grandmother on Dad's side have a

small farm in British Columbia. That's the reason we went there a couple of years ago. We don't see Grandad Sydney or Grandma Imogene very often because they don't have the money to visit, and neither do we. We live only about eight hours away by car, but that's how cash-strapped everyone is. Things are better than they were a few years ago but still aren't great. Dad says, *Once you get behind, it's hard to set yourself straight.*

When we went there, Grandpa and Grandma took me horseback riding one day. I had a saddle on my horse, but they didn't because Grandpa said, *They're a pain to put on.* We trotted our horses along the pine-scented woods, and when we crossed a stream, cold water splashed against my legs, tickling them, but I never got soaked. Flies buzzed around us. I remember swatting at them. The horses seemed equally annoyed, as they swung their tails around in an attempt to get rid of the *pests* as Grandpa called them.

Mom and Dad didn't come with us because Grandma and Grandpa only had three horses. They stayed back at the house, and when we returned, I remember Mom and Dad sat closely together on the old porch swing as we came up the path. Dad had his arm around Mom's shoulder, and they were laughing and drinking iced tea that Dad had made. Mom drank it, but Grandpa and I both thought it was terrible.

Grandpa said, *Robert, what are you trying to do? Give me diabetes in one glass of iced tea!*

Grandma Imogene said, *Well, at least he makes an effort. When was the last time you made iced tea?*

Grandpa Sydney smiled, and said, *I cook!*

Grandma replied, *You, barbecue! Anyone can burn stuff!*

The memory of Grandma and Grandpa makes me laugh. They're funny and kind, with big hearts. They would do anything for us. When we were having money problems a few years ago, Grandpa thought about selling the farm and giving the money to Dad and Uncle John. Uncle John would have taken it, but Dad told Grandpa on the phone, *That's silly. You have to live somewhere, Dad. And anyway, there's not that much money in the farm. Just take care of yourselves, alright?*

Dad helps Grandpa do his taxes. That's how he knows how much money the farm's worth.

My parents, sitting and laughing side by side, with Dad's arm around Momma—that's my favorite memory of them.

As long as I don't look down, I don't feel nauseous. If I relax and sway with Enisseny's motion, and try not to fight it, it's soothing. It's almost as if I'm being rocked to sleep. Bob has his head on my lap now and has relaxed, too. Bob's eyes begin to open and close with the motion of our flight. I'm sitting upright, against the edge of the dragon's talon. Enisseny, for no reason, tightens his claws around us, blocking out the wind. Warm in the center of Enisseny's palm while I dream of Mom and Dad, me and Bob drift off to sleep.

CHAPTER 7

"Jayden," a voice says softly. Hands rock my shoulders back and forth. I rollover. When I place my hands on the ground, the dirt stings them as if I had put them on broken glass. I sit up, rub my eyes, and attempt to focus on the young man who's in front of me. He has curly brown hair that sits on broad shoulders, but in comparison to my dad, his shoulders are narrower.

I blink a few more times in dazed confusion, wondering where I am and why this guy is standing over me. I wonder where Mom and Dad are.

Then, I remember the last week: the news I overheard in Mom and Dad's bedroom, the fight with my parents, and me leaving them to see Wyndham and the dragon. Finally, after so many years of never meeting the dragon and the knight, I had gotten the chance. Now, Wyndham is missing because of that Hunter named Osgoode.

Canonsland. That's where I am.

As I stare at eyes that stare back at me, I know who this guy is. It's Laurence.

"Are you alright?" he asks as one shaking hand rests on my shoulder.

"Yes," I answer, as my eyes sweep across the area in search of Bob. I crane my neck, peering through the darkness. Night has already moved in. As I place my hands on the ground again, finely diced stones dig into them, leaving behind small dents in my palm.

I stand up and make my way around a corner. I quickly step backward, take a deep breath in, and quietly yelp, "Cliff!"

Two white moons cast light illuminating the landscape before me, and because of the bright glow, I see blood-red water that's surrounded by a black mountain. Part of the mountaintop is what we're standing on.

In the ocean, there are random sinister rocks that jut out of it. If a person were to fall from the cliff, there's a good chance they would be killed on the rocks. Or, they would be killed when they fell into the ocean. My eyes shift a bit, and my mind fumbles as I almost lose my balance. I take another step backward.

"Enisseny!" Laurence turns and hisses. I glance over at Laurence and follow his gaze upwards. Above us, the white dragon stands with his white wings extended as he peers down at me and Laurence.

"How could you? Wyndham will run his sword through me when we find him, and he sees that we brought small Jayden!"

"I'm not that small! I'm eleven, for Pete's sake!" I say, throwing my hands up in the air as if I'm asking the two moons to help me make this guy understand. I add, "Stop thinking of me as a kid! I'm not that much younger than you," I growl at him.

Laurence spins around. "I am seventeen, Jayden! *You are a child.* Wyndham said as such before leaving when his last words were: *Take care of the child.*"

With Laurence's words thrown at me as if I were a slight annoyance, he raises his eyes again to Enisseny and whisper-shouts, "Come back down here, Enisseny! They will see you!"

The way he dismissed everything I said causes something to explode inside of me. "Listen to me!" I shout. I run towards Laurence and yank at his arm. "Why does everyone think I'm a kid who doesn't know anything? I know stuff! I know my family's poor! I know Momma and Daddy are sending me away because Momma has cancer! I know that she might die—just like Grandma Nettie! And I know that I may never see Wyndham again—because he's already dead!"

The reality of the words hit me. I can't unsay them. My eyebrows instantly slip down, and my tummy hurts. I've said the words.

Momma has cancer. Wyndham may be dead. If my life were a glacier, it's as if part of the iceberg has broken off and fallen into the ocean, making the water rise. A good chunk of my foundation has collapsed.

Someone has turned the tap on again. This time, though, it's been cranked up all the way. The water hits my face like the red waves hit the rocks below us.

Laurence's face becomes stricken as he stares down at me. A moment later, he kneels down on his knees in front of me, places one hand on my shoulder, and says with a half-smile, "Jayden, Wyndham is fine. I am sure of it. He may need a little help from us; that is all. Now, what do you say of your mother?"

I choke on tears, gasp, and say, "Momma has cancer."

"She is sick?" he asks.

"Yes," I answer. "People die from it where I come from. Grandma did."

"Does everyone?"

I wipe my nose with my sleeve, sniffle, and shake my head, no.

"Well, then," he says. "Wyndham has said you love your parents immeasurably, and you worry about their welfare. I would say … why not hope she is one the illness will not take?"

A small smile crosses over my lips. Maybe I'm wrong. Another six years might make Laurence wiser.

His words also mean more to me because Wyndham told me that Laurence, his brothers, and his sister lost their parents when they were young. If he can be hopeful on my behalf, I guess I can, too.

"As for Wyndham, we have seen him come back many times when we had all but given up hope. I would ask that we not think the worst until there is a reason to do so. Enisseny has not." He gestures, pointing up at Enisseny on the cliff.

"How do you know he hasn't given up? He won't come down," I quietly say.

Laurence glares upwards at the dragon. With his lips tightly closed in what might be frustration, he says, "The dragon refuses to come down because he is angry with me."

"Why?" I ask.

"I scolded Enisseny while we were traveling here for gathering you and Bob up from the fields of Rumbling Town. Wyndham's escape will not be easy. There will be danger. Wyndham gave us clear instructions to ensure you were both safe while he was away."

"Oh," I say as I raise my eyes to Enisseny.

He didn't leave us behind. The white dragon refused to do it.

"Don't worry, Laurence. I'll tell Wyndham it's Enisseny's fault—that you had no choice. Where is Bob, by the way? *And where are we?*"

"I saw Bob scaling the rock towards Enisseny. We are at Red Ocean Pass. It is where The Hunters lived more than two hundred years ago. It is their home."

"Why are we here?" I ask while raising my right hand and rubbing it on my forehead.

"I do not know, Jayden. Enisseny brought us here."

"Come, we should climb to where Enisseny is." Laurence swings a bag out from behind his right shoulder, reaches into it, and pulls out a rope. Then, he ties a knot around my waist and his waist.

"What are you doing?" I ask.

"I swear, Jayden, you are here now, so you are coming with me. But if something happens to you, Wyndham will not care if he calls me brother … or son. He will have my head."

I giggle at him. Laurence's face stretches out in a smile. "You are not afraid of heights, are you?" he inquires with raised eyebrows.

With my fingernails clasped tightly against the edge of the black slippery rock, and my body pushed as close against the mountain as I can in a clear signal that I am terrified, I quickly release my fingertips from the outcrop, step forward a bit, and say, "No, not at all."

"Good." He smiles. "Let us go."

The trail around the cliff is made up of loose gravel that, when I walk, slips under my feet, making it treacherous as we weave along the side of the mountain. My feet slide beneath me, and at one point, I nearly call the Red Ocean my grave when I'm almost hurtled into the water below us.

It's Laurence who pulls me back.

At several spots, the trail is wide, and we can easily walk side by side, but in other parts, the stretches are narrower and make it difficult for me to walk, but even more so for Laurence, because he's bigger than me. Laurence has one end of the rope tied to my waist and the other end to his. He says, *if either you or I fall, we will leave this world together.*

As we continue to climb upwards, the wind picks up and whips against my face with the cold air but also causes the rocks to fly up and scratch my cheeks. I raise both hands in protest to the wind and the rocks, but also to protect myself. We reach a spot where we turn a corner, and in front of us is a boulder that blocks the path.

Laurence stops for a moment. He then pushes it gently, and with one small yank, we see it become unbalanced as it wobbles back and forth. He turns to me and says, "Do not step on the rock, Jayden."

The rock is large. I watch Laurence step around it with his long legs, and he slips effortlessly to the other side of it.

"How am I going to do that?" I ask him. "My legs are too short."

Laurence pokes at the boulder in front of him again, and it teeters. He then pulls out a flat-faced wooden hammer and a hook from his bag and begins to drive it into the side of the mountain. I watch him untie the rope from around his waist and expertly fasten the line to the hook, tying it off in three knots.

The wind howls, the sea crashes, and Laurence's words come to me in splintered fragments. I hear him say, "I'll swing you over the side of the cliff and pull you up."

"I'm not doing that!" I scream at him. "Why can't I just step on the rock?"

"It will shift and may cause other rocks to come loose. We will be caught in the middle of a rock avalanche."

"You don't know that for certain!" I retort.

"You are right. But I prefer that we do not take the chance."

Eustace told me about his little brother, Laurence. Eustace said each of them is special in their own way. Alwyn is the oldest and is the responsible, follow-the-rules kind of man. Constance is, as her name suggests: She is constant and a woman that can always be relied upon. She is a perpetual presence of grace, warmth, and kindness. Eustace, by his own definition, is good at bringing all his siblings together, even if they don't always agree. He said: *I am good at bringing harmony to our family— 'tis my responsibility.*

That's why he was talking to Alwyn, and in no uncertain terms, I was to butt out.

Laurence? Laurence is a whooooole different person. He wants to be a knight like Wyndham, someday. Eustace said: *The youngest of all of us, he fears nothing. Not sea, nor wind, nor swords. He had escaped his older brother's sight many times when he was to tend to chores. The boy, when not doing as he is told, can be found climbing rocks all alone.*

I bite my lower lip. Laurence doesn't know that I know this, but given that Eustace had said this, and not him, I think I can trust Eustace's judgment. If Laurence believes it's unsafe, *there's a good chance it is.*

"I'm afraid," I confess in between sniffles.

"I know," Laurence says softly. "You will be fine. I shall not let you go."

I sit down on the edge of the mountain. My legs hang over the precipice. I peer around the boulder in front of me, and I notice that Laurence has tied the rope to the hook, but he has looped it around his shoulders as well.

"Jayden, are you ready?" he asks.

"Not really," I mumble.

Laurence turns away for a moment. When he faces me again, he gives me a crooked smile and says, "You said you were not afraid of heights."

"I lied," I say as I glance up at him.

"Then, make it true," he says while raising his chin and eyes in my direction as if he were challenging me.

I fill my belly, taking a deep breath in, close my eyes, and use my hands to push down on the edge of the cliff and lift myself off.

As my butt slips off the ledge, there is a sudden lightness under my feet. For a second, my tummy flips upwards and then downwards, as I quickly begin my descent.

CHAPTER 8

There's a swirling sound through the air. My legs kick through nothingness. Hands are outstretched as my knuckles scrape against the side of the rocks in front of me. I'm desperately trying to grab hold of something.

I'm facing the rock. Moment after moment, I watch a blur of black shadows slip past me in a rush before my eyes! It feels like forever as one section of the mountain goes by, then another. I'm still reaching, but there's nothing there.

I hear the whirl of wind as I fall. Suddenly, a high-pitched squeal cracks through and shatters the sound of my descent. The shriek rings in my ears like an ambulance siren. Terror ripples through me, heightening my emotions as if my skin were pulled back when I have a cut, and I feel everything more intensely: cold, dampness, and heat. And if someone, or something, jabs me in that spot, it's so painful that I instinctively pull the sore away from whatever is hurting me.

I want to stop this fear. But I can't.

I'm desperately, painfully, frighteningly aware "the squeal" that I hear—it's me!

With a *swoop*, I bounce once. Swiftly after that, there's the sound of a *whack,* and then a *crack* as my head punches the rock in front of me.

"Aww!" I shriek. I stick my hand out in an attempt to prevent any more hits from the rocks. Once I've stopped bouncing, I dab my palm to my forehead. When I turn my hand over to analyze it, a sticky red mixture is smeared into it.

I'm bleeding.

I've stopped falling. For a few seconds, I swing back and forth. My legs sway with the wind. I continue to keep my hands in front of me for protection. I swear those rocks are really trying to hurt me.

"Jayden, are you safe?" I hear rushed words come from above me.

Below me, raging water swirls around, slapping across jagged black rocks that poke out here and there close to the shoreline.

I yell up to Laurence, "NO!!!"

I slip a bit further down and grab hold of the rope that's in front of me. Thank God, the line that Laurence tied is still secured around my waist. When I was falling, it was the only thing that stopped me from going all the way down.

That is, once Laurence decided to grab the rope again.

A deep, chuckling sound comes from above me. I kick my legs in the air, while tightly gripping the rope. I half-heartedly convince myself that if I hang on to the line in front of me, it will stop me from crashing into the ocean and rocks below, even if Laurence decides it would be fun to let go of his end again.

I know it sounds stupid. But right now, it's the only control I have.

My teeth are clenched together as I yell, "Are you

laughing?"

"No, my dangling child. Surely, not," he says this while roaring louder with laughter. I slip further down the side of the mountain.

"Laurence! I'm falling!" I screech. At the same time, my voice is husky, and my words come out as if they were washed over by the water below me.

"I will not let you fall, Jayden. You have my word." His words are said with a sudden, serious sound of an adult, and with concern.

I bounce once just like my Slinky would do on the stairs when I was little, and then I slowly rise. My fists tighten around the line, and calluses form instantly.

Laurence heaves me up the side of the mountain, and I bump along it scraping my elbows and my knees. I know I shouldn't do it, but I can't help myself, and I glance down below.

Beneath my feet, I watch as water crashes on the shoreline. I visualize a thousand ways I could die. The most obvious way I can see my death is by falling and landing on one of those rocks. I stiffen up, and my legs begin to tremble. Even if I did make it past the rocks, there's a good chance the ocean would swallow me up.

Does Canonsland have sharks?

"Pull me up faster!" I order, Laurence, as I begin to swing myself back and forth. My teeth chatter. I seem to have summoned more wind with my swinging. It was already cold, and now it's freezing.

"Jayden! You are truly not helping your plight!" he bellows down to me, and I notice immediately I've stopped moving upwards. "Stop swinging! For the love of all great things! If you wish to help, use what strength you have and pull yourself up with your arms, while also planting your feet firmly on the rock in front of you.

Pretend the side of Mount Lieuschanean is nothing more than the road in front of you. Do this, and if you pull yourself up, you are able to walk up the side of the cliff. On this end, I, too, will pull you up."

I can tell his teeth are clenched together as he says this to me. The words come as sounds that are louder and softer with small grunts that are scattered throughout the sentences.

I stop swinging for a second and hang there. *I'm petrified!* It really makes me mad that Laurence thinks he's in charge of me. After all, he's only six years older. But I need him to help me. I guess it wouldn't hurt for me to try to do what he says.

My hands grip the rope. I place both my feet on the side of the rock in front of me. Slowly, I begin climbing, as instructed by Laurence.

A few minutes later, I'm close to Laurence. I can see him now. He shouts to me, "One moment, Jayden. I must tighten the slack."

I stop as instructed. Pushing backward, I watch Laurence take the excess rope and tie it to the hook. He's back now and leans over the edge. With his hand outstretched, Laurence says, "Take my hand, Jayden."

I reach my hand out towards him, and then I see something.

Or, someone.

Osgoode is standing right behind Laurence. His sword is out! Osgoode's red-faced and drenched in sweat. He looks angry. With the light from the moon, I see bruises and several cuts that crisscross his face, and he's wearing the same clothes when he left with Wyndham. There's one big difference, though: The colors smeared across his shirt are a mixture of brown-black mud with an accent of red.

"Behind you!" I scream and let go of Laurence's hand.

I am once again free-falling along the side of the cliff, and in desperation, I clasp the loose string tight, tighter, and tighter still, as I fall, fall, falling ….

And then I'm jolted in an instant upwards again, and for the second time, I hit my head against the rock wall.

This time, it's different for me. I don't check for bumps or scratches, or to see if I'm bleeding. I begin a much faster ascent to the top with the instructions Laurence has already given me. I'm terrified that Laurence has been killed. But if he's alive, I'll help him. I don't know how, but I will.

If Laurence is gone—

I sniffle a little and realize I'm unarmed and alone. Not that I know how to use a weapon. But a knife, or a bow and arrow, or something, might give me the smallest advantage to defend myself and Laurence if he's injured. With the strain of pulling myself up, my arms begin to burn, my legs are on fire from all the effort, and I slow down climbing.

Then, I stop.

It's all too much. What's happened to Laurence? This rock in front of me is too big to climb up on my own because I'm too small. I'm terrified of heights, AND I'm afraid of falling. As I look down below me—I know, I don't want to drown, either.

Wyndham is missing. Mom is sick.

Swaying back and forth in the air, I close my eyes. I hang there for a few moments letting the wind push me around. Nature can do what it wants to me. Whether I fall or drown, I'm tired of being scared.

I blink my eyes open. Looking up to the ledge where I saw Laurence a short time ago, I tightly clasp the rope, bear down on the rock, and with newfound strength race up the cliff through tears, hiccupping, and whimpering. Forcing the tears back, I scream, "Ahhhhhh!!!!!"

If I were a warrior in some legendary battle, I would consider it my last-stand cry. It's the scream of: *I WILL NOT BE DEFEATED!*

Then it occurs to me: *WHERE ARE BOB AND ENISSENY? OFF, SNIFFING THINGS TOGETHER? Laurence and I could really use their help right about now!*

When I reach the top, I breathe out a huge sigh when Laurence pops his head over the side of the ledge.

"Are you alright?" I say in sharp, quick words.

"Yes," he answers as he pulls me up.

As I wiggle my butt up over the side, I see Osgoode has the rope wrapped around his shoulders. His sword is tucked away in his belt.

"Ahhh!!! I scream and charge at Osgoode with my hands balled up in fists. "WHERE'S WYNDHAM?" I shout. I punch him in his arm, chest, stomach—wherever I can!

"Jayden! Jayden! To my surprise, at the words that you uttered, I let go of the rope that was holding you," Laurence says as he pulls me off of Osgoode. "It was Osgoode who reached for the rope first and took up the position that you now see him in. For certain, if he meant to kill us, he would have made swift work of it with my distraction and you in a perilous state. I think it best we should hear what he has to say," Laurence says as he lets go of me.

Osgoode stands back and says, "I understand if you believe that I have deceived you. I came to see Wyndham for the purpose I said. But it would seem others used me as their puppet for another plan that they did not share with me." His eyes look down at the ground and stay there for a few seconds too long.

Laurence and I both look upwards to where Enisseny was perched.

But Enisseny is gone!

"Lord Fulke," Laurence mutters between his teeth as he shifts from leg to leg. He probably would be pacing right now, except we're standing on a narrow part of the trail.

"Yes," Osgoode answers. His eyes stare down at the black, dusty stones.

"Has he taken the white dragon?"

"Yes." Osgoode's eyes won't meet Laurence's. I notice Osgoode's hair is long and greasy, but even in the darkness, I can make out the faint lines on his face that show his age with the light from the moons. I guess him to be about the same age as my dad, probably in his forties.

My tummy bounces like it did when I was hanging over the cliff. "Where's Bob?" I ask Osgoode.

"That is your dog?" Osgoode asks.

"Yes," I answer with an unintentional huff of frustration.

He says, "I do not know. I was almost upon Enisseny and quickened my pace to protect the dragon. I saw Enisseny and a dog peer down over the cliff. I do not know what would be of such keen interest to them, other than to watch perhaps over two people they care for. But the dog was the first to hear the wizard, Droart, suddenly appear behind them. He gave quick barks and yelps to threaten the intruder. Droart would not leave, and I saw your Bob clasp his teeth around the foot of the wizard that serves Lord Fulke." Osgoode winces and says, "Droart kicked his foot into the air. Bob's teeth were still tightly clasped around his leg. The poor animal flew from the force of the kick and hit a single tree that sits at the top of the mountain." He looks down at me and continues. "Some spell was cast on Enisseny, and for that reason, he could not help Bob. Under the wizard's magic, Enisseny allowed Droart to climb on his back, and they took off in flight together. I spared a moment to search for the dog but could not find him. Then I heard your cries and hurried here to help. I am sorry, Jayden. I do not know where Bob is."

He moves back to Laurence, staring at him with dark eyes, and asks, "Why did you come? Wyndham and I were together in the dungeon. He said the white dragon would be safe. That he had made it clear to his family that they were to protect the white dragon, and the child, Jayden, above all else." Osgoode lifts a hand and waves it in my direction when he says my name.

Laurence won't make eye contact with me. Instead, his gaze is fixed on Osgoode.

I'm trying really hard not to cry over Bob. I know we have to find Wyndham and Enisseny right now, and that some people have said to me and my parents that *Bob is just a dog.* But they don't get it: Bob's family to me, Mom, and Dad. My parents have even said Bob is like another child to them.

"Wyndham was gone for a week!" Laurence's words come out as if a bomb exploded. "What would you have me do? Wait for him to be returned in pieces?"

"You went against the rest of your family?" Osgoode asks.

I stare at Laurence. Even though Osgoode *seems* to care about what happened to Bob, I don't trust him. I'm trying to subtly communicate to Laurence that, if he tells Osgoode there's only the two of us, he could have us captured, too, if he's lying to us. For all we know, he could be deceiving us right now. This could be another trap.

Laurence's eyes focus on Osgoode as he says, "No,

Enisseny brought us because the rest of my family are leading an army. We were sent ahead to see if a war could be avoided. We will take Wyndham back, whether through words or by force."

"Then, it will be by force," Osgoode says in a whisper as he turns away from us. When he spins around again, he says through tears and a deep voice, "For there is no one here to speak with. All those who wished to settle the land and try to live by peaceful means by farming orangeberries, danstauds, red corn, and flastudus are no longer. You see, there is no one else left—'cept for me."

Osgoode's voice began as a distant soft rhyme. But as he explained what had become of the rest of the farmers, his eyes grew darker, and his words were louder and sharper. It was a different man that stood before us now from the man who saved me a few minutes ago.

Osgoode was shaking with anger.

"'Tis good news an army is coming," he says as he moves close to us and places a hand on Laurence's shoulder. "Come with me. We will fetch Wyndham from the prison and be ready to fight by the time the others arrive. There is no reason to take the treacherous path that my people have laid out for trespassers that would lead to a quick and painful end on the rocks below," he says as he gazes over the side of the cliff.

He steps in front of me and Laurence and says, "For there is another way. Some ways weave and fold within the rock, filled with stairs that would take you one way, and lead to nowhere. But if you choose the right direction, you may navigate your way out to the tower that contains the dungeon, to the entrance to my village, or to the top of the mountain. I never knew this place as a child, but when we returned some months ago, we carried a map and found our way. I know all the paths well now. I can take you to Wyndham in a short time. For that is how I arrived here to help you and Jayden, with all but a few moments to spare before Jayden—"

I hold my hand up to him and say, "Yeah. You don't have to finish that sentence."

Osgoode gives me a small smile. When I turn to look at Laurence, he's grinning from ear to ear.

"Come," Osgoode motions with his hand and swings his head in the direction we should follow him. He then walks a few feet and places his hand in a hole, and the rock instantly rolls out of the way—the stone that Laurence determined was "loose" and could create a "rock avalanche."

I scowl at Laurence, point at the rock, and say, "Are you joking?"

Laurence shrugs his shoulders, sticks his hands out to both sides, and says, "How was I to know?"

I cross my arms in annoyance with Laurence's *expertise*. Then I turn in a huff and follow Osgoode, with Laurence behind me. As we pass the rock, my eyes widen at the view in front of me when we enter the cave. Behind us, there's a swishing sound of levers tugging, and then the rock that let us in swiftly seals us inside the mountain.

CHAPTER 9

Except it's not really a cave. Caves are dark, muddy, and cold. Inside a cave, I know that different types of critters will sleep there: such as bears that hibernate in winter and bats that hang upside down.

I love all sorts of animals. Mom will take me to the library, and I'll grab ten books on rhinos, elephants, and even bugs! But sometimes she'll make me put some books back. A few months ago, she wagged her finger at me and said, *Jayden, that's too many. You'll lose track of them. We don't want to pay any late fees.*

I said to her, *I've never lost a book! And we've never had to pay late fees!*

Mom squinted at me for a moment and then said: *We did last year.*

It was one time, and only the once. I'm really good at taking care of my things, but Mom remembered. I frowned at her when she reminded me. She smiled, put her arm around my shoulder, and said, *Baby, I only brought it up because I know my little girl is perfect most of the time. But even you make the odd mistake.* Then she paused for a moment, softly smiled and said: *Besides, there's a good chance your father would forget to drop them off. And because of him, we'd have to pay!*

We both laughed. It happened once when Momma gave Dad the library books to return, and he put them on the back seat of his truck. He drove around with them for almost a week before she asked him if he had returned them to the library. Dad stared at Mom with his mouth open for a few seconds and said, *Oh, no!*

Yup, we had to pay late fees.

Anyway, from all the books I've read, I know the Earth is a big world with many animals that live in both hot and cold climates. There are polar bears and beluga whales that live in Churchill, Manitoba, and in the desert, you can find scorpions. In Africa, there are lions and rhinos!

But if I had to choose, the best animal that I know is my dog, Bob. And, the most different I've ever seen is the dragon, Bob!

Is he an animal? I don't really know.

Or, I mean Enisseny. I've been here for over a week, and I still accidentally call him Bob. Constance said: *Don't worry about such things. You have called him Bob for many years. It will take as long, if not longer, to remember he has a different name.*

Constance was leaning forward as she said this to me. Her skin was white like milk, and it glowed a bit, and she had rose-pink lips that turned gently upwards at me. She even smelled like roses. Then I remember that we both had looked over at Enisseny.

Enisseny was so close to us, his breath was warm on me, and every time he moved his head, he created a small breeze. After she said that, Enisseny gave me a gentle push with his black nose, and he blew both warm and crisp cold air at me from his mouth. He blinked a few times at me. I was in a trance and just stared at him.

It was as if everything else had fallen away: Constance who stood beside me, Wyndham, who had left, and for a few moments, I even forgot that Mom was sick. Time was suspended. The dragon's eyes, his breathing, the way he stared at me, it was as if he understood our whole conversation—and some things that were never said.

Wyndham had left five days earlier, and Enisseny had been okay with it. But the next day, Enisseny wouldn't eat his food, and his talons clicked against the stone floor as he paced back and forth in his room in the castle. Every now and then, the dragon would hit the wooden door with one of his legs. It was as if Enisseny were trying to gently kick down the door. It was pretty clear he wanted to leave.

On day seven, well—Laurence, took care of Enisseny's problem.

"What do you think?" Osgoode asks.

"This is not a cave," I say as I squint up at him.

Osgoode's face contorts. He places his hands on his hips and swings his head back and forth as if he's trying to make his own assessment. After a few minutes, he says, "For certain, 'tis."

I reach up and touch the light blue color of the cave wall in front of me. A wet, dewy mixture of crumbling stone falls to the ground. Green ferns grow in the cave, and trees with sapphire-colored leaves hang above the shrubs. There is dark black soil beneath my feet, and my boots sink into it. This makes me curious, and I bend over to examine the dirt more closely. I pick it up, turning it over in my hand the way Dad does when he studies the soil. The path outside the cave is made up of rough stones, but as I turn the dark mixture over in my hands, I notice it's damp, smooth, and thick.

This soil is healthy and alive.

All around us, water flows. Birds fly above us and sing their songs. A purple bunny with big floppy ears pops out from around the corner and peers at us. He's almost as big as Pup!

Laurence mumbles, "Has this always been like this?"

"Not always," Osgoode answers. "I never saw this as a child as my people left hundreds of years earlier. They never considered returning as they believed the land was spoiled and would never return to the way it had been. I imagine when they left, this part, too, was ruined. But my parents, at bedtime, would tell me stories of my lost home and the way things had been long ago. They described the cave in vivid detail in the way I see it now. But I did not believe them. For me, it belonged to the realm of fantasy and fairy tales. I know now, I was wrong.

"We returned here in the last few months, at my insistence, because we could not find a new place where we could set our foundations. When we returned, we carried a map with us that would help us find our way into the city and avoid the treacherous route along the outside of the mountain. Imagine our glorious joy when we entered here and saw this! We knew the soil was rich again. At this point, my people splintered into two groups: those who wished to return to farming and peace, and others who wished to fight."

"I do not understand. With a bountiful land, and your home reclaimed, why would your people not want to enjoy that which was returned to them?" Laurence asks. His voice sounds high-pitched with an edge of frustration in it.

Osgoode stands still for a moment, staring at Laurence. Uneasily, I glance back and forth between Osgoode and Laurence as I twist my hands together and begin to bite my lower lip. There's a pause…hanging in the air. Osgoode shifts his right and left foot back and forth as if he's dancing with no one. Hands are placed on his hips, and then he quickly relaxes them and drops them back down to his side.

There's something Osgoode doesn't want to tell us. I know it.

With an exhale, I watch Osgoode's chest push out, and he says, "The other group, the warriors, wished to seek revenge on those who did not help us in our time of need. When I was but a child, I was told that when we first set out hundreds of years ago, when our land was drought-ridden, and we could no longer grow things, and then our livestock perished, we asked to share the land of others. With each town that we approached, we were turned away. After some time passed, those who led my people realized it was futile to ask to join other towns, and we turned to bows, arrows, cannons, and swords to take that which was not ours."

Osgoode stares at Laurence and says, "You have heard of this last part. Rumbling Town was one of the villages that we did dare take."

I'm confused. Wyndham said that they overused the soil, and that was the reason they were unable to grow things. He also said that they hunted everything in their area to extinction. I stare up at Osgoode, my face twisted at him. My eyes squish together from the pressure of not being able to understand why Wyndham had told me one thing, but now Osgoode was saying something different.

Osgoode's eyes are locked on me, and he asks, "What perplexes thee, Jayden?"

"Well," I start, "Uhm …."

"Go ahead, child. I do not bite," he says with a smile. In spite of all the dried blood on his clothes, and the mud, and the cuts that crisscross his face, it's a kind smile.

I try to put the words together in a non-argumentative tone, so I don't offend Osgoode. We still need him to show us where Wyndham is. Also, overall, Osgoode seems like a good guy.

I stare at the ground. An orange bird flutters to my feet. I choose my words carefully and say, "Well, uhm … Before Wyndham left, he told me the story of your people. But he told it a little differently," I say while twisting my hands together. I casually glance over at Laurence. I'm hoping Laurence will help me figure out how to tell the story that I know. If Wyndham spoke to me about it, he must have described the Hunter's history to Laurence, too. After all, Laurence is a knight-in-training.

"Yes," Osgoode says.

I swivel my head around in Osgoode's direction.

"'Tis true. We overused the land. Once the soil would not yield food, and our livestock died, we killed all the animals that roamed close by us. But, at that time, there was a drought that devoured the whole of Canonsland, as well. We were ordered by the King to ration our land, and thereby also our food. We were to share amongst ourselves. Some farmers would be permitted to produce one year, and then the next year, those farmers would be forbidden from farming. If you farmed, it was expected you would share your harvest with those who were not permitted to; and then the following year, when a farmer was not allowed to grow a crop, the favor would be returned. But we did not heed the King's advice. We did as we wished. In turn, we destroyed the land, our livestock died with no food to eat, and then we hunted to live."

Laurence again shifts from foot to foot. His eyes dart around from Osgoode, then to me, and finally to the fluttering leaves on the trees. His hand is placed casually on the hilt of the sword that he carries. I don't know if that's intentional or not.

After a few moments, Laurence gazes down at me and says, "Jayden, 'tis no reason for Osgoode's people to suffer so long. They made a mistake in not heeding the King's advice. But, for certain, a mistake made does not mean that they should be forced to roam Canonsland for so many years without a home, and to worry about how to feed their young."

Osgoode's face becomes void of color, and his hands relax at his sides. He raises his eyes to Laurence and says, "Laurence, do not think I share the opinions of our warriors of today. Remember, I represented the Hunters who wished to farm. I wish to say, though, on behalf of my people, I am truly sorry for all that was done to Rumbling Town by my forefathers."

My lower lip trembles. I focus on the lush dirt on the ground. My mind races as I recall everything that Osgoode has told us. I've tried not to think about it, but now I have to. Everyone he loved has been killed because they didn't want to go to war. They wanted to live peacefully. And, they were punished for it.

Please don't be mean to him, Laurence. Be kind.

Eyes are resting on me. I sense them on the back of my head, but I don't want to look up. I can't. I hear the words, " 'Tis a long time ago. Well before the start of my life, or that of my parents. There is no need to apologize for the sins of your ancestors." Laurence's voice comes out in shaky waves with words that catch on one another and sometimes are pushed together hurriedly.

Laurence hesitates and continues, "Besides, I do not know if my people would have shared their land with others if they had been asked. I like to think they would have been different."

I raise my head. My lower lip shakes.

Laurence moves in closer to Osgoode, who was standing quite a distance away from us. Laurence says, "Truth is, I do not know. People are, at times, greedy, even if they are blessed with an abundance of rich land, water, and shelter. We do not always care about others who suffer. Truly, we can be better only to those who live now." His voice is filled with sadness. But is there something else?

Is it failure? Regret that the people of Rumbling Town didn't help a long time ago? It seems odd that two men stand here now, who are taking responsibility for stuff done by their people before they were even born.

But maybe it's needed so that everyone can move forward.

He places his hand on Osgoode's arm and says, "Come along, friend. We will find Wyndham together. From there, we will decide what needs to be done."

Osgoode chokes. Then, I watch as he drops his head onto Laurence's shoulder and sobs for a few seconds there. I can't watch him cry. I turn away. Quietly, tears fall down my own cheeks, and I quickly swipe at them. I don't want Osgoode to see me with tears. I know it might make things worse for him.

A moment later, Osgoode lifts his head and says, "Look at me. I am sorry. I do not mean to be so weak."

"Yes, I would say you cry as loudly as the child, Jayden!" Laurence emphasizes the "child" part in a playful tone.

I'm sure he's kidding. It's something that Dad would do. "Hey!" I smile. "I've told you once, and I've told you twice, I'm not a child!" I chime in. I watch both of them as they bend forward in laughter.

I place my hands on my hips, signaling my impatience

as I turn my lips to the right and begin to tap my foot while I say, "If you boys are done *bromancing*, can we get on with finding Wyndham?"

I like being in charge, even if it's just pretend.

Osgoode and Laurence swing their heads back, slap each other on the back, and continue laughing at me.

"Okay," I instruct, "everyone follow me." I lead them in the direction that we were heading before we had that *squishy moment. Dad would not approve.*

"I suppose we should do as she says," Laurence says, gesturing in my direction to Osgoode. There's a small pause, and I hear him continue with, "The little one is now in charge."

I haven't looked back. Because if I did, I would have to admit I have no idea if I'm going in the right direction or not. Besides, I hear footsteps behind me, and that means they might be following me.

All I hear for a short time are footsteps: definitely mine and one other set. But I don't think two people are following me.

A few seconds later, I hear, "Jayden?"

I stop in my tracks. Laurence, who was following too closely behind me, steps on my heel, and I turn and scowl at him. Then, I glance over at Osgoode. He hasn't moved from the place he was before.

"Perhaps, we should go this way," Osgoode says as he points to the right.

"Oh, okay," I answer. "Well, maybe this one time, you should lead the way." I giggle.

"I would be honored to lead you, my lady," Osgoode smiles and bows to me. He takes my hand as I approach to help me over a slippery rock. Once safely across it, he lets go.

From behind me, comes a deep snickering. I squint at

Laurence and shoot him dagger-eyes, and he instantly
stops laughing. We fall in line as we were before, with
Osgoode leading me, and then Laurence.

A few minutes later, Osgoode says, "Of course, before
we continue, you must answer one question for me."

I grin and reply, "Anything."

"What is the meaning of the word that you just
spoke?"

I'm dumbfounded and ask, "What word?"

From behind me, Laurence says, "I do believe he
wishes to know the meaning of the word "*bromancing.*"
And for that matter, I wish to know as well."

"Oh," I say. I get flustered, as my face turns red. "It's
a word for men that have a very close friendship. They're
almost like brothers; they get along so well. It's two men
that are inseparable."

"'Tis, not so bad," Osgoode says, as he winks at me.

"I agree," Laurence echoes with a smile.

Ruff! Ruff!

"What's that?" I ask. My heart races with excitement.
Can it be Bob? I'm so terrified of being disappointed.

Laurence and Osgoode exchange a cautious "look"
between each other. From their expression, I know they
don't want me to be hopeful either. Just in case.

Then, I hear shuffling in some bushes, another *ruff!
ruff!* And before I have to worry, another moment that it
might not be him …

Bob bounces onto me, knocking me to the ground! I
giggle, rubbing his head with so much love as I clasp my
arms around his neck. He wiggles out and then comes
back, and now his disgusting, kibble-breath drenches my
face in wet slobber. I'm rolling around on the ground,
trying to push him away, and then grabbing him again.
Bob won't let up.

When he's had enough of me, he runs over to Laurence, and then to Osgoode, leaping on one of them and jumping on the other, as he whimpers and cries at the joy of seeing all of us. I'm laughing so hard my ribs hurt, and I shake from too much happiness.

And I'm crying, too.

Once we've had our reunion and Bob settles down, we begin to walk. Osgoode is leading the way, sort of. Pup is racing ahead of him, but every now and then, he stands on a rock, or further up the path, and waits for us. He never lets us out of his sight.

"You have an extraordinary dog, Jayden," Osgoode announces to me.

"I know," I whisper.

"Come along, Jayden," Laurence says, and he takes my hand so that I don't slip as we walk carefully down green, slimy stairs.

Together, we make our way towards the tower with the dungeon that holds the prisoner that we all love.

His name is Wyndham.

CHAPTER 10

My heart thuds in my chest. Pup is panting. Bob seems to know that we need to be quiet as he slinks along beside us.

It's this place. When you think everything is beautiful, there's always something that keeps you unsettled. I like knowing what to expect. That's the reason I love jigsaw puzzles. If you put the pieces together correctly, you will have a picture that makes sense. But this place? It's as if someone put the wrong part of the puzzle in the wrong place, and the sky is where land should be.

We left the Garden Cave, as I like to call it, as the sun rose above us. We managed to manoeuver our way along by running from bush to bush without being seen by the guards and are now only a few feet from the tower. The tower is this grey-black structure that sticks out from the rest of the landscape. It's been abandoned for so long that trees, vines, and grass encircle the black prison and whisper together. Or, maybe what I'm hearing are the sounds of long-dead prisoners who haunt the tower.

I'm sure there's an echo of something.

According to Osgoode, the tower is made of black

rock from the mountain. For this reason, both the mountain and the tower add darkness to what is an otherwise bright landscape. Surrounding these two objects is lush green grass dotted with red and pink roses and various blue, white, and yellow flowers that stretch across the field and cling partway up the side of the tower.

The red ocean terrified me at night because it resembled blood. But when the sun began to rise, I noticed it was more of a coral color. I know what coral looks like because Mom has a beautiful blouse that Daddy bought for her one Christmas, and that was the word she used to describe it. She wears it whenever we go out for dinner. Most of the time, dinner is generally at McDonald's. Dad jokes with her: *You're wearing your best clothes for our gourmet dining experience!*

I sigh deeply. *I miss home.*

I watch the flowers sway in the wind. Pink, purple, red, and yellow dots are attached to the tower, and I scrunch my face at them. *They're flowers.* They shouldn't be anywhere near an ugly black building where prisoners are kept—especially when one of the prisoners is a generous, heroic, kind knight like Wyndham!

"There are four guards at the tower. Two of them are outside; two remain inside. We need some distraction for the two outside," Osgoode hisses at us. "I shall jump out; then, the guards will chase me. You and Jayden run for the tower and find Wyndham."

I'm sitting back listening to this, and it doesn't make sense. *We need Osgoode.* He's the only one that knows his way around the tower and the dungeon where Wyndham is being held. He's also the only one that can take us back through the Garden Cave.

Lawrence frowns at him and says, "The guards will

remember you were captured, held in the dungeon with Wyndham, and you escaped. I am certain they will kill you instead of chase you. And we need you to lead us back through the cave."

Oh, good. For once, Laurence and I are on the same page.

"I shall do it," Laurence announces as his chest puffs out like the rooster on our farm.

I roll my eyes.

I watch Osgoode's face become accented with lines as his eyebrows come together. He says, "You are the only one amongst us who has trained with Wyndham. You know how to use a sword. I think there will be a good chance we will need it."

I'm leaning against a rock. The rock is hidden in bushes where me, Laurence, Osgoode and Bob sit and consider what to do. It's a good hideout for a short time. But, with all this arguing over who will be a distraction, it seems we have a better chance of getting caught way before we find Wyndham in the tower and free him from the dungeon.

Laurence and Osgoode continue with their back-and-forth. I've stopped listening. They've completely forgotten about me and Bob being here. Bob looks up at me. It's as if we're both thinking the same thing. I take one glance back over to the tower. Through the bars at the lowest level, two eyes seem to peer out at me. I'm not sure the eyes see me, but that's enough of a push for me to make the decision I do—without consulting Laurence and Osgoode.

I wiggle away from the rock. Before I know it, I'm running up a hill in the opposite direction. Every now and then, I will lunge as quiet as I can into bushes where I can hide to catch my breath and to rest at different times.

Bob, to my surprise, is doing the same thing. He's become a little commando dog, as he hunches down and stays out of view.

I knew I couldn't pop out at the exact location where Laurence and Osgoode were hiding. Otherwise, I would have given away their hiding spot. Once I've decided I'm far enough away from them, I stand in the middle of the path and scream, "Ahhhh!!! Help me! A bear is chasing me!"

I sprint along the path with my dress twisting around my ankles, and from behind me, I hear, "Chyld! Chyld! Stopp! Stopp, I sayz! What's this, ya say? What is ay boar?"

Oops. I guess bears don't live in Canonsland.

I slow down a little and look to my right. I pretend I see a big grizzly bear, and I begin squealing again and tear off further down the path when a bush conveniently begins to move. Don't know what it was, but to whatever critter was in there, *thank you* for moving at that perfect moment.

One guard who was closer to me, jumped back a bit when one of the bushes shook as I pointed at it. The other guard, a taller and heavier man, lagged further down the path, but he leaped back, too.

I hear huffing that's so close, it sounds like it's in my ear. Bob is so far ahead, I can't even see him.

Good dog.

I'm ripping along the path with stones flinging from my shoes. Then I hear a voice.

"'Tis sad, when a child can run faster than grown men."

I know that voice.

Upon hearing the man's words, the two guards stop in their tracks. I stand quite a distance away. When I turn around and see the man, I take a quick breath in that causes me to become light-headed. My tummy lurches. A shiver runs through me when I recognize him.

It's Alwyn.

He's a farmer; he can get hurt! And I've seen him run, too. Just like the guards, he's not very fast.

I slowly start walking towards the soldiers and Alwyn. Out of nowhere, hands grab me, cover my mouth, and lift me up. I am pulled into a tree that has a hole in the bottom of it, and I'm dragged inside.

A second later, I'm turned around, and with a finger to her lips, she says, "Shhh …"

"Constance!" I quietly whisper. I'm so relieved I swing my arms around her to hug her, and my fingers get caught on her long flowing blonde hair. She is bunless. Behind her, I see Bob sitting back, his tail swishing behind him as he happily watches our reunion.

As I look at Constance, I notice she's red-faced, huffing, and she smells like a horse. Her white shirt has more of a yellow color to it with crusty, dry mud splattered in random places throughout it. Constance isn't wearing a dress or a skirt. Instead, she's wearing brown pants. The dirt doesn't show as much on them because of the color, but in examining them closely, I see small dots sprayed along the fabric. Her riding boots come up to her knees, and it's covered with crusty muck that breaks off and mixes with the dirt on the ground.

Thunk! Thunk!

Whirl, smack!

I stare at Constance with my mouth open. Then I begin to twist my hands around in my skirt. *What were those sounds?*

Constance places a protective hand across my tummy, holding me back. Then she pops her head out from the tree to get a better look. I wiggle close beside her and stick my head out, too, but I stay a little further back.

I want to see, too.

Standing on the path is Eustace, who holds a raised sword above one guard that was standing in front of Alwyn, and now is laying on the ground at his feet. A little way down the path, the other mammoth guard is sprawled out in the middle of the road with his arms and legs stretched out in the same pose, as if he were creating a facedown snow angel.

Laurence sprints past the facedown-snow-angel-sleeping-guard. In his hands, he holds a slingshot that he clutches. Constance takes a few seconds to scan the area quickly and then clasps her hand tightly around mine, and we crawl out from the hole of the tree trunk together. Constance continues to hold my hand as we walk towards Alwyn.

"Are you mad, child? You could have been killed!" As Laurence approaches, he hurtles the words at me with as much force as I suspect he used when he hit the other guard with the stone.

"You are not one to say such things to Jayden! You also do not do as you are told, but do only what you wish to do!" Alwyn snaps at him. "I know you wish to be a brave knight. But now, you are a lost young man. If you do not learn to do as you are told, what hope do you have of becoming a great knight like Wyndham?"

"Do not speak of Wyndham!" Laurence spits the words at him. "You have never been fond of him. You, so keen when we were young, you were convinced that you could care for us, and we did not need him. I remember what you said! You would be happy if he were gone!"

Quietly, we all stand aside as we wait for Alwyn's

response to Laurence's challenge.

Alwyn folds his arms together in front of him and moves in closer to Laurence. They're inches apart when Alwyn says, "Yes. You are right. I believed I could care for my siblings on my own when our parents died. I did not know then what was required to care for one child, let alone three. I believed I knew much more than I did and did not need the help of an old knight, who was never a father. You see, Laurence ... I can say these things because I was but a lost young man, too."

Laurence's mouth is open, but no words come out. In an instant, the lines on Laurence's face smooth out; there's calmness to it that I haven't seen in the last week.

"Besides," Constance's words break the silent spell we're all under, "we watched you for some time. How long had you planned to hide behind that bush? How much time do you think you would have had before the guards saw you and Osgoode?"

Constance and Alwyn are my new heroes. I don't need to explain stuff to them.

With that, Constance surveys the area and says, "Where is Osgoode?"

Just as we're all beginning to wonder the same thing, I see Osgoode walking up the path. Following closely behind him, I see one of the guards. Constance steps in front of me. Laurence frowns at Constance's reaction and swivels around on his heel. When he sees the guard, he yanks out his sword. He pushes Osgoode aside, and in one swift motion, places the edge of the sword against the guard's throat.

Osgoode steps in front of the guard and says, "This is my one-time friend, Toly," he announces. He hesitates and says, "He helped me escape from the dungeon and was part of the warring group, but he has had a change of heart." There's an extended pause, and then Osgoode adds, "Toly, set me free when he caught sight of Enisseny."

"Why did you not mention him before? And why did he not set Wyndham free as well?" Laurence shouts at Osgoode as he takes a small step backward while lowering his sword.

"I feared that you would not trust me if I told you that I had help from a guard. As for Wyndham, he was weak and said I should go alone. He could not even stand," Osgoode says, as he clenches the muscles in his cheeks and sticks his chin out. "I believe Droart may have poisoned him."

"We waste time talking. I was to check with the two guards posted outside of the tower to confirm that all was secure and report back to Godfrey. If I do not return soon, he will know something is amiss," Toly chimes in. "We will miss our chance to free Wyndham if we do not move with haste."

Osgoode says, "I can tell you about Toly now, because your siblings have arrived, and I know you said they were summoning an army. Even if I lied to you, we would be outnumbered. But, as I am on your side, I am relieved." Osgoode's face relaxes for the first time since we first met, and he continues, saying, "I'm sure the soldiers wish to help us free Wyndham. Where are they? Are they hiding on the other side of Mount Lieuschanean?"

From beside me, I hear Constance snap, "That is what they said? That we were bringing an army?"

Osgoode's face noticeably turns red, even underneath the mud and dried blood that is splattered across it. Small droplets of sweat run down the sides of his face and gather in his sideburns. I can't help but wonder if he's sweating from all the running, or from trying to protect his friend, Toly.

At that exact moment, water droplets drip from my nose, too. I suspect now from my own sweat, it's probably a combination of everything.

Osgoode's face lowers in the direction of Constance, and he stammers, "Ye-ye-yes."

Constance flicks her eyes over at Laurence, then back to Osgoode, and says, "An army is coming, but they have not arrived. When my brother released the dragon on his own, he did not know we were coming with one. He took it upon himself to free Enisseny and to seek out Wyndham alone."

Laurence's shoulders roll forward, his chin lowers, and his eyes drop to the ground. But as he lowers his glance, his eyes catch mine.

I look away.

I hate moments like this. When someone you like is genuinely trying to do the right thing but breaks a couple of rules and gets in trouble for it. Okay, it hasn't been a smooth escape plan, but still ….

"His heart was in the right place," Eustace says. He places his hand on Laurence's shoulder and continues, "You left to find Wyndham, but you did it alone. We are family, dear brother. We are always on your side, even if it seems like we are not. We love Wyndham as much as you. He is both father and brother to us. It would have been better had you spoken to us before you freed the dragon and went off on your own. You see, brother, Alwyn, and I had already sent word to the King and told him of Wyndham's disappearance and Enisseny's sudden change in mood. I understand you grew weary from waiting. You must understand, though, at that moment, I was in the process of speaking to Alwyn to see if we might go ahead. But, before I could discuss the matter with him, you had released Enisseny, risking the life of the dragon and the inhabitants from other realms."

"This is lovely. But, truly, we must go." Toly swings his head out from behind the right side of Osgoode's shoulders. "There is one guard left. If I do not return, he will sound the bell. If the bell is sounded, many more guards will come. It will make Wyndham's escape much more difficult," he says, with impatience stitched into his words.

Osgoode moves in closer to Constance, and says, "How is it that the child and the dog came to be with Laurence then? Wyndham said that they, along with the dragon, were to be protected."

Constance smiles as she answers, "Enisseny. From what I heard, Enisseny gathered them in his palm and carried them away. Neither Laurence, nor the dragon, bothered to do as they were told."

"The dragon knows that you must be here." Osgoode's words are said boldly, as he glances in my direction.

Constance proudly puts her arm around my shoulder and says, "Yes, Jayden was needed as a distraction."

Osgoode and Constance laugh together. Everyone else smiles, and we watch them.

"Tick, tick …." Toly raises his eyes to the sun while pointing at it.

Okay, maybe not everyone is smiling.

We laugh at Toly's joke, all except for Alwyn. He grabs Laurence's bag and pulls out some rope while saying, "Okay, knightly brother, do bind the soldiers' hands and legs. Make sure the knots are tight, and they cannot escape."

"We will need two people to stay back with the guards that are captured. Eustace and Constance?"

"Certainly," Eustace answers without hesitation.

Constance nods her head.

"Jayden," Alwyn turns to face me. He kneels down, scoops my hands into his, and says, "I would ask that you stay back as well."

My face heats up. I sputter at Alwyn, "It's because I'm a kid, isn't it? You don't think I'm important? You think that I'll just get in the way? That I can't do anything right!"

Alwyn leans back as if he's been scorched by fire. But he doesn't let go of my hand. Quietly, he says, "No. That is not the reason. I believe you are very important, and that is why I wish you to stay with Eustace and Constance. I wish you to be safe."

Alwyn's words are soft like Daddy's were when he talked to me about Mom … When Dad pleaded with me to stay with Grandma and Grandpa for the summer and told me what an adventure it would be, to be somewhere different, and how going to the Okanagan Valley would broaden my horizons—force me to meet new people.

Dad was just trying to protect me. No one told me that Mom was sick and that while I was away, she would be getting treatment. Dad said that night in the conversation I overheard but wasn't meant to hear: *You'll be all better when Jayden gets back. She may never need to know.*

I'm always fighting with people and argue with them about this stuff. And maybe this is one of those times when I need to step back. Everyone needs to focus on getting Wyndham out.

I take a deep breath in and hang onto Alwyn's fingers. I sigh and say, "Okay."

Relief spills across Alwyn's face. He nods and says, "Good."

"Are they secured, Laurence?" Alwyn asks as he

simultaneously lets go of my hand, and leaps to his feet.

"Yes," Laurence announces.

Laurence carries one guard on his back to the cave. Alwyn, Eustace, Toly, and Osgoode struggle to lift the second guy. He's enormous. When he stands, he's taller than Laurence and also is very muscular. When we are back at the cave, me, Eustace, Constance, and Bob hunker down in it.

I'm restless, though, and I know I'm not needed to watch over the two sleeping guards. So, I stand up, walk to the entrance of the cave, and watch as Toly, Alwyn, and Laurence stroll down the path together. Osgoode is alone again and hangs back from everyone else.

For no reason, Osgoode spins around and stares at me, as a pair of dry, small hands are gently placed on my shoulders at that exact moment. Even though I'm pretty confident I know who it is, I raise my eyes and see Constance. She glances down at me for only a microsecond and then lifts her head to watch Osgoode.

There's something there—something that makes me feel unsettled. It's as if I should leave.

Osgoode gives us a final wave of his hand, and me and Constance wave back to him. Then we watch, as Osgoode jogs forward a little to catch up to the group. My shoulders are squared slightly to the right, and this allows me to watch Constance and Osgoode at the same time.

Constance and Osgoode are so far apart. Yet, there's something there.

Respect?

Or is it something else?

I chew my lower lip and wonder: Is this what it looks like when two people are falling in love?

CHAPTER 11

Jayden remains protected in the cave with Eustace and Constance, who are also tasked with watching the two prisoners. Laurence, Alwyn, Osgoode, and Toly put their plan in place to free Wyndham. Always skeptical, Alwyn remains doubtful of the Hunters' sincerity in helping to liberate the knight:

I do not trust Osgoode and Toly. They have put my family at risk, in particular, my youngest brother, Laurence.

The youngest of my siblings, Laurence, is an arrogant young man who flaps his arms in battle and puffs his chest out. It reminds me of the brightly colored pegster birds that behave in similar fashion to woo females. But for Laurence, there is no good reason for such behavior, except to prove he is the bravest and the fiercest fighter in all of Canonsland.

He is a reckless boy.

Stop scowling at Laurence, Alwyn, Eustace has said to me many times.

My answer is always this: *The boy is always so keen to go charging into battle alone. If Wyndham does not instruct him properly on how best to survive as a knight, he will be killed in a few short months after he becomes one.*

Eustace and I have many fights about young Laurence.

Eustace is different. His gesture and mannerisms are those of a diplomat. He should look for a life in politics. His mind is such.

Most days, Eustace's words do not bother me but work well to ease my mind. But as I recall these past conversations now, my face reddens much as wood that is scraped together to create a fire. Water droplets form on my brow, and I place my hand to my forehead and wipe them away with my palm. The sensation of sticky perspiration drips down my back as well. The uncomfortableness of sweat adds fuel to my already hot temper.

But Eustace sees things in Laurence that I do not. He has said, *Laurence may be many things—impertinent and impatient are two—but he knows the mind of people well. While at times, his emotions rule his thoughts and actions, he's got a good sense of who to trust and who would deceive him.*

As we approach the tower together, Toly whispers, "Osgoode and I will enter first. I will hold my sword to Osgoode's back as if I have recaptured him. Laurence and Alwyn, you follow behind. One guard remains. It will be enough of a distraction in seeing the recaptured prisoner that the guard, Godfrey, will not challenge me. There are many corners in the tower and therefore many places to hide. Find the right spot, and do what you must to the guard. So long as he does not reach the bell and summon the others, you will be able to escape with Wyndham before anyone knows. If he rings the bell, we will find ourselves in a difficult and outnumbered position. There will be many that will come; we are four and Wyndham."

"Do you trust him?" I say, turning to Osgoode. "Your life and ours now rest in his hands."

"I do not know," Osgoode says. His voice is flat and barren, as this land may have looked two hundred years ago when it was drought-ridden, and the Hunters were forced to abandon their homes. "But, as far as I see things, there is no other way. We will know in a short time whether Toly has reclaimed his senses, and now knows he was on the wrong side of things."

Toly's eyes and Osgoode's eyes rest heavily on each other. It would seem a challenge has been put forward to Toly.

A moment passes between them as they stare at each other. Toly is the first to break his eyes away from Osgoode's, as he pulls some rope from his belt and ties Osgoode's hands. "Is that loose enough? If you need to, would you be able to free yourself?"

Osgoode calmly nods and says, "Yes."

"Let us go then," Toly commands as he walks behind Osgoode as if he is his prisoner. Laurence and I follow behind them. After a few moments, I notice Toly raises one hand to the left side of his chest and holds it there. It's as if the guard wishes to calm his heart by placing a hand on top of his chest. Then Toly, slowly removes it.

***

We inch our way along the tower walls—Laurence and I. From behind the pillars, we observe as Toly and Osgoode march in. I glance back at the way we just came, mindful that we may be followed, or that Toly has told us some story in the shape of a lie and guards are lurking in the shadows waiting for the right moment to capture us.

Osgoode's head is bowed. He does well in playing the part of the prisoner.

"Good day, Godfrey. Look what I found skirting the tower."

"You've dun well!" he shrieks, while his voice crackles

101

in a most venomous way. "Perhaps, Lord Fulke will let you keep yer head?" He bends forward with a fluid-filled lungful of laughter, and then he suddenly chokes. Raising a hand, he coughs into it, trying to clear his passage.

Osgoode's head hastily pivots in the direction of Toly's face. His face turns white as if he were a ghost.

Up until hearing the words spoken by Godfrey, Osgoode was convincing in his role as a captured man. But with Osgoode's quick glance at Toly, his white face, and mouth open, he clearly shows he cares for his friend. If I were the guard, I would be concerned. But this Godfrey does not seem to notice, as he continues to babble on about random things to no one.

A sigh passes over my lips. If Osgoode is not careful, he will give away the rescue of Wyndham—whether intended or not.

"Perhaps," Toly answers. Then he casts a quick glance in the direction of Osgoode, and a sinister smile passes over his lips. "How is the prisoner?" Toly asks of Godfrey

"As gud as can be expct'd."

"Watch him." Toly barks at Godfrey, while gesturing to Osgoode. With that, he swings a little steel plate back, and his eyes peer into the room. He says, "Why, Wyndham, you are not such a mighty knight now, are thee? You, sprawled on the floor there, all bloodied. It turns out the man hath no power. His power only is with his beast."

The guard, Godfrey, roars in laughter and smacks Toly on the back.

I spin to face Laurence. He would not be happy with what was just said about Wyndham. I am a moment too late. My hand slips through Laurence's elbow as he takes off running.

Laurence roars with a sound that I cannot explain. His feet charge forward in the direction of Godfrey, Toly, and Osgoode, his sword waving in the air. I fall forward in my attempt to stop him.

I mumble, "The boy has a wish for death, I am certain." I drop my head for only a second. Then I chase after my little brother, as I have always done.

The view before me is tumultuous. Toly swivels around too late, and the guard, Godfrey, with a rounded fist, knocks him across the face. Toly slides down the door to Wyndham's prison and collapses on the floor. Osgoode runs a distance away from the fight and hides behind a pillar where he feverishly tugs at the ropes that bind him. I am not certain whether I should follow my baby brother or help Osgoode. I say a small prayer and whisper, "I hope Wyndham has taught Laurence well." Then I rush over and pull at Osgoode's ropes for only a second, and then remembering I carry a small knife with me, I remove it, and after some effort, I slice through the ropes, and Osgoode is free.

I spin on my heel, ready to help Laurence. But I cannot move. I stare at my youngest brother, as I watch Laurence and Godfrey begin a sword fight. Their feet dance here and there, and the ringing sound of swords echoes and sings within the hallways of the tower.

Toly is slumped along the prisoner's door. From behind the door, I hear a familiar voice, "Toly, you must free me! I know that to be the boy, Laurence!"

The sound is one I knew well as a child after my parents died. *It is the voice of Wyndham.*

Osgoode and I run towards Toly, while Laurence and Godfrey continue their sword-step-dance. In truth, when I have a moment and see my little brother, I must say he knows much about sword fighting. When I find Toly, he is starting to come to, and I grab his shirt, shaking him, and shout, "Where are the keys to free Wyndham?"

Osgoode bellows, "Give me thy sword that ye took from thee! I must help Laurence!"

Toly hands Osgoode his sword, and the now sword-wielding Osgoode runs to Laurence's aid. Toly uses my shoulder to brace himself and rises to his feet. He wobbles around the corner and emerges with a ring of keys.

Toly struggles with the keys for a second and finally takes one out. The door swings open with such gusto from the other side that it knocks Toly backward, and he is now sitting on the ground for the second time in a few short minutes.

Osgoode stands behind Godfrey with his sword out, while Laurence is in front of him. Godfrey is attempting to take on both of them at the same time. Once Wyndham is out, I watch as Toly throws Wyndham his sword, and he takes his place beside Laurence.

Laurence smiles upon seeing Wyndham and says to Godfrey, "You are surrounded. You must surrender else you will die!"

Godfrey's devilish eyes dart around to all of us. His frame is plump, and I catch a whiff of the drink called wysemore that oozes from his pores. Everything about him, from his sputtering ways to the way he looks at us, says that he means to end our lives.

"I shull nev'r giv'up!" he yells in our direction. "How'd dar you, Tolee! You know the cost that Lurd Folk will cast upon or vill'ge. You've betray'd us," he says with a judgemental finger outstretched in Toly's direction.

I had not noticed that Toly is leaning against the wall. His head is bent forward.

"You are right," he says, raising his eyes to Godfrey. "I

104

have betrayed many of my people. And, yes, I know the cost. But I am no longer convinced Lord Fulke will fulfill his part of the bargain," he says with words that seem more quiet with each one said. In truth, Toly appears smaller now than only a few moments ago. I watch him closely for fear he may disappear before my eyes.

With newfound strength, his head jolts up, and he continues, "Lord Fulke has forced us to kill our own people!" he shrieks in the direction of Godfrey, standing with closed palms and outstretched arms.

"What is this?" I say. "Killed your own people?"

Toly stares at me and says, "Lord Fulke ordered us to kill those who wished to live by peaceful means, as they were the ones also who would not go along with Lord Fulke's plan to capture the dragon. They were the people who followed Osgoode.

My eyes sweep across towards Osgoode. The man's eyes are moist with grief. I flick my fingertips together; my mouth opens, then closes.

I have no words.

Godfrey's face is reddened from the drink, the fighting, or perhaps from the words just said. Godfrey says, "Lurd Fulke—He'd kull us all! Rescul. We cannot win agn'st that!"

Rescol.

"What is this?" Osgoode's eyebrows are bent forward. He looks at Toly. "What does he say?"

Toly stares at his one-time friend with a small smile that lines his mouth. But the smile is not of arrogance, I do not think, nor from a man who plans to betray us.

"Rescol," Toly answers. "The illness that swept through Rumbling Town some years ago. It killed three-quarters of the town before the dragon stopped the spread of it. We heard of it," he flutters one hand in my direction and adds, "For certain, you are old enough that you would remember?"

I stand frozen in my place. Unable to speak, I nod. *Our parents were taken because of it.* In a few short moments, my world has spun out of control. The Hunters killed their own people, and now I wonder ... was Rescol Lord Fulke's creation that killed my parents all those years ago?

My eyes swiftly move towards Wyndham. I wait for him to answer the unspoken question.

Wyndham's glance is broken as he briefly looks at me. With downcast eyes and a long sigh, he says to Toly, "I remember it."

"You know how it came upon Rumbling Town?" Toly asks in a manner that says he may already know.

"I do," Wyndham answers. He keeps a watchful eye on Godfrey and says, "'Tis Lord Fulke and Droart."

"Yes, the wizard Droart cast a spell on the man, and he became ill. Then he unknowingly passed it to the people of Rumbling Town," Toly finishes.

Wyndham shouts, "Droart is a man, not a wizard! I spoke to the man who said some clear liquid was driven into him with a needle. He became ill a short time after that. There is magic in this land, 'tis true. Enisseny possesses it and a few others! But it is not as often as ye wish to believe!"

Wyndham's words tumble out of him with such rage, I can barely keep up. I've never seen Wyndham like this before.

He continues, "Droart is a doctor in mixing things. So long as we prevent Lord Fulke or Droart from injecting a person with some venomous needle, there will be no return of Rescol!" he roars at all of us, and to no one in particular. He's silent for a moment and then adds, "The King and I. We had no proof. The only person who knew what happened was the first to die. I have spent all these years waiting to catch Lord Fulke in some other transgression."

I was angry for a moment at Wyndham for not telling us the truth. But now, I understand.

"I do nut bel've yu," Godfrey responds. "As wul, thy've captur'd thee dragun. If the dragun hath magic, Lurd Fulke hath it naw."

With these last words spoken, Godfrey charges towards Osgoode. Osgoode slaps his sword a few times as a defense. Once he is past him, Godfrey runs around the corner.

There is no more time for words or to figure out what has or has not happened. We run along the corridors in pursuit of Godfrey.

"Where has he gone?" Laurence shouts. All of us are spinning around in circles in hopes we catch some sight of the rotund guard.

Toly's face is white as he follows us with breath that is labored. "They will know you are here. You must leave now if you wish to have a chance at life. He will ring the bell. Other guards will come."

"Why did you not tell me of the illness?" Osgoode shouts at Toly.

"We needed you to fetch Wyndham. I did not know that Wyndham would come without the dragon. We hoped that once Wyndham was here, he might have a plan to help us stop Lord Fulke from unleashing the illness on our people ..." His voice breaks off. His eyes linger on the grey stone floor for a long moment.

When Toly looks up, he says, "I did not know that we would be forced to kill our people. There were only a few people at the beginning, one or two who lost their lives in skirmishes. We needed to make it believable that there was a risk of war. But I did not know all who preferred your way would be killed—and we would be the ones to do it. I cannot tell you how penitent I am." Toly says with eyes that have reddened.

At that moment, I believe all that has been told to us.

"Where has Godfrey gone?" I ask.

"There are secret passages in the tower. And there are many. Many of them lead to the tower bell."

Wyndham grabs a sword that is leaning against a wall and shouts, "Toly, Alwyn, and Laurence take a secret passage. Just pick one!" Wyndham says while throwing the sword in Toly's direction.

"Osgoode and I will go up the stairs. We will take the route that is expected."

***

We weave our way along the dark passage, with Toly lighting lanterns when we come upon them. This is more dreadful than scaling the path along Mount Lieuschanean that Constance, Eustace, and I were forced to travel because of Laurence. The way is littered with webs and rats the size of Jayden's dog. Every now and then, a black rodent runs across our boots. Sometimes, we come across some grisly remains of a prisoner where all that is left is a skeleton in clothes. Their mouths are wide open; it's as if their last breaths were a scream.

As we reach the top, I'm grateful to see the light again. But my happiness is undone when I see what is in front of us. Wyndham and Osgoode are doing their best to fight five men: Godfrey and four others that we have not seen before.

When we come across the other guards, Toly turns to me and Laurence and says, "I did not know!" Then, he charges forward and begins to fight one of the guards, with Laurence following closely behind him.

I am horrified when I watch Godfrey slip away from the skirmish to ring the bell. I chase after him and pull my sword out to stop him. As I climb the stairs to the next level, I hear behind me the grunt of a man. Concerned that I have lost my brother, Wyndham, or Osgoode, I quickly glance down to see Laurence standing above the body of one of the guards. A few moments later, Wyndham ends another guard.

Laurence, Wyndham, and Toly all fight the last two guards. They are quite skilled with a sword. While I stand distracted on the stairs, Osgoode rushes past me to prevent Godfrey from ringing the bell. Suddenly aware again of what needs to be done, I race up the stairs behind him. When I reach the top, I fight with Osgoode against Godfrey.

For a round man, he certainly is good with a sword. Our swords cling together. But I lose concentration and stumble backward. Godfrey stretches forward, slicing me along the arm and then not a moment later, runs his sword into my chest. Red blood sprays in all directions from my wounds.

Osgoode looks down at me and then screams, "AHHHHH!!!!" He recklessly charges towards Godfrey.

For me, it is over. I slump backward, falling to the ground.

I drift in and out of this world. Small snippets of remembrance are sprinkled before me: as children, chasing two-year-old Laurence across red-yellow meadows; playing with sticks with Eustace; laughing with my sister, Constance, over something; my marriage in the pouring rain to my beautiful Idonea; Petronilla, giggling the way she does at nothing; and crying as I watched my mother's face turn from a ghastly white to a grey color, and her lips turn blue when she left us, and to witness again a short time later when my father died, too.

My eyes are back in this world, and for a few brief seconds, I watch Osgoode fight, Godfrey. Osgoode stumbles back, too, like me, and then Toly appears suddenly, stepping in front of Osgoode …

When I wake again, Osgoode holds Toly in his arms, as blood streams from his chest. I force my eyes open a little longer. Toly's eyes are wide as he gasps and utters the words, "PLEASE FORGIVE ME." His eyes still wide, he raises his head a little more, as if he's trying to catch his breath. Then, Toly's body stretches out for a moment, and the wretched struggle he was fighting ends.

I begin to drop off to sleep once more, but my eyes roll open to the sound of church bells ringing. In these last moments, I have time to consider moments of regrets: things I have said to Laurence; and words I never spoke to Idonea, Petronilla, Constance, Eustace, and Wyndham.

Toly's words are the perfect ones, I decide as Laurence wraps me in his arms. I whisper to him, "*PLEASE FORGIVE ME.*"

With that, my eyes close, and darkness surrounds me.

CHAPTER 12

The King arrived with his knights and soldiers. We found out they were here in a terrible way—one of the men slipped off the cliff.

I heard a man's scream, and my heart thudded inside my chest. My legs sprinted towards the entrance of the cave, as my mind spun around, thinking it might be Wyndham. Before I could get outside, though, Constance chased me and grabbed me by the elbow; she stopped me and said, *Eustace, will see what has happened first.*

Eustace found the man's body, returned briefly to grab a blanket used for one of the horses, and placed it over the dead soldier. Meanwhile, Constance kept one eye on me so I couldn't leave, and a sword against the two prisoners from the tower who finally woke up.

Once Eustace returned, he forced one of the prisoners up. With a sword to the man's throat and blood vessels bulging in his forehead, Eustace shouted at the man, *show me the way through! Or I shall end you here!*

Eustace is the calm one of all the brothers. In the last week, I never saw him lose his temper, except for today. The prisoner was hesitant at first to help. He told us Lord

Fulke had threatened to kill his people by unleashing Rescol on them if they didn't help to capture the dragon.

Eustace and Constance's faces turned white for a few seconds when he said this, and they stared at each other in confusion. But Eustace told the prisoner, if he didn't help the King's men, the Hunters would never be free. After all, the King and his men came to help them because they were told about the civil war that was brewing amongst the Hunters, and to stop it from happening, they brought an army.

The prisoner said, *Ye lie. Thee King cum to rescue Windem and the drugun.*

Eustace laughed, rubbed his nose, and said *the King is fond of Wyndham, 'tis true. But do you believe he would risk so much for one man?* He paused and then continued, *as for the dragon, you are right, the King would move the world to free him. But the King does not know the dragon is captured. Enisseny was free when last he heard.*

The prisoner gulped and paused for a moment. He choked on his words and said, *I will show thee the wayy. But ye must prumise me y'll help my people, and save them if ye can frum Rescul.*

We will do all that we can. Eustace said, as he took a step forward towards the guard and stared at him without moving a muscle.

I didn't know.

I didn't know that's how Alwyn, Eustace, Constance, and Laurence lost their parents. Well, I knew they died because they got sick. But I didn't realize that it was the wizard Droart that made the townspeople sick, that Lord Fulke was behind it, and that it was called Rescol.

But neither did Eustace and Constance.

Eustace and Constance are furious now because they know Droart and Lord Fulke killed their parents, but also on behalf of the Hunters. Constance said quietly to me, *it was such a terrible thing to see: to see someone you love die from Rescol.*

Eustace and the guard left, and when they returned, the King and his men were with them. But, a few seconds later, a bell sounded from the tower. The King remembered stories told to him as a child about the Hunters; when the bell rang in the Hunters' Tower, it meant more guards were coming. The King, the knights, and the soldiers all raced towards the tower. Me, Eustace, Constance, and a few of the King's soldiers waited in the Garden Cave, while everyone else left to help.

I'm standing outside the cave, and as one of the returning knights passes by me, I touch his arm and ask, "Sorry, do you know if Wyndham is alright?"

I hold my breath, and my chest tightens as I wait for his answer.

He smiles. For a second, I don't know if it's a smile of pity because he might have to break bad news to me, or if it's because Wyndham is okay.

The knight says, "He is free."

I am so happy, and then ….

"Alwyn!!!!" From far away, Constance screams out, and it instantly shatters my happiness. The scream rings in my ears. It sounds like church bells that calm the nerves, but this is the opposite of that. I want her to stop screaming because the sound is breaking my heart in combination with her shocked face, where all the lines have fallen away. I cover my ears to block the noise out.

I can't tell what's happened. But I know it's something terrible. In reaction to Constance, I'm pulled in and follow her mood. My heart pounds, and the hair on my arms stands up straight as my stomach begins to ache.

Then I watch as her brown boots kick up grass and dirt, and she flies faster than Enisseny did when he carried me and Bob in his palm. I don't want to see, but I do. I stand on my tiptoes, and that's when I know what's happened.

Osgoode carries Alwyn across his shoulders.

I'm leaning against the wall of the cave. I don't know what to do. I watch as Eustace takes off after Constance, and several of the soldiers run behind them. I begin to run after them, but one of the knights that just returned pushes me back against the wall and says, "Child, do not go. You do not wish to see it." As he says this, he holds me back.

More of the King's soldiers run towards Alwyn, and they bring blankets. Osgoode gently places Alwyn on the ground. A few seconds later, Constance, Osgoode, Eustace, and several of the soldiers lift Alwyn up and set him on the makeshift stretcher made of bedding. Then, Eustace, Constance, and the soldiers run with him on the blanket-stretcher into the cave.

I kick the knight and try to squirm out of his grasp, but it's no use. I form my hands into little balled fists and punch him as hard as I can, while screaming, "Let me go!"

Constance and Eustace's faces are void of any emotion as they pass by me, but their red-rimmed eyes give away their sadness. As they pass, Constance briefly glances up at me, but she doesn't notice me. I am a ghost to her. Alwyn's head also lifts up from the blanket in my direction. Then, as if it's all too difficult, he lays it flat against the plaid fabric a second later. Everyone disappears into the cave.

With the knight's hands firmly on my arms, he says to another man, "Have they taken him to the King's doctor?"

One of the guards says, "Yes."

With that, he releases me and walks away. I'm still standing against the cave wall. Now, it's just me and Bob. I slide down against the bumpy rock, and it scrapes along my back. I notice it, but barely, because I don't care. Once sitting, I wrap my arms around my bended knees and quietly cry into them.

Bob moves in and licks my head, my cheek, and if I try to cover my face more, he moves in even closer and catches whatever piece of me he can with a kiss: whether it's my hand, eyelash, my ear, or just the side of my cheek. Bob won't leave me alone, because he never does. I eventually lift my head and say, "Bob," and wrap my arms around him and hang on tight like I've always done when things get too hard.

My face is buried in Bob's fur. A hand gently touches my head. Then there's that voice I know, and it says, "Jayden?"

I raise my head. *It's Wyndham.* I'm happy. But my lower lip trembles and dinosaur-sized tears tumble down my cheeks. Wyndham wraps his arms around me, lifts me up, and carries me into the cave as I sob into his shoulder. I pop my head up to make sure that Bob follows us, and when I see he's right behind us, I lay my head against Wyndham's shoulder again.

***

Wyndham carries me for some time and holds my head. I settle down a little bit, and then he plops me down on a tree stump. The King and his men are some distance from us, but we're far enough away that they probably can't hear us.

"Please forgive me, Jayden. My intention was not to bring you here to meet my family, and then to watch

115

them get hurt, and to witness the start of a war unfold in Canonsland."

"I know. But why did you bring me here?" I ask. I fiddle with my hands as I glance up at Wyndham.

He looks terrible. His beard is longer now, and there's dried blood in it. Across his face, there are specs of red dots. Wyndham's white linen shirt is nearly brown, and it reminds me of how I must have looked when I was four years old and played in the mud with my imaginary friends. (My imaginary friends were Betty and Sally, and we were the three amigos. We would go shopping together, have tea, and bake cakes for Mom and Dad. But they were mud cakes, so Mom and Dad always thanked us, but they never ate them. I can't blame them.) Wyndham's shirt is torn in places, and there are bruises around his eyes. He's also a lot thinner.

Wyndham stands in front of me, though, and even bruised and bloodied and with his clothes torn, in his eyes, he's still Wyndham. But there may be something different in those eyes. Anger? I don't know. Wyndham speaks to me in a calm voice.

He stands beside me and says, "You did not wish to go to your grandparents. I thought if I brought you here and showed you that traveling somewhere different can be an adventure—where you have the chance to meet new people and see different things—you might be more willing to stay with them, as your parents wished you to do."

I twist my hands around in front of me and stare at the ground. Then, I start tugging at my dress.

"Mom and Dad are sending me away for a reason," I mumble, without looking at Wyndham.

Wyndham's eyes are on me. I know it. He begins tilting down a bit, and then a little bit more.

I quickly look up at him, and he's right there, smiling at me.

I can't help but giggle. Even with everything that's happened, Wyndham's still joking around.

"You will always be forced to deal with me, Jayden. I always win. Even at something simple, such as avoiding my eyes."

I laugh harder at him.

Wyndham continues with his smile. It's the calm one that's permanently splashed across his face. Then he asks, "Do you wish to tell me the reason?"

I've only been on a roller coaster once in my life, and it was exhilarating, terrifying, and sometimes while I was on it, I wanted to cry. I was laughing a few moments ago, and if I were on a roller coaster right now, I would consider that the climb up to the top of the hill on the ride. But this moment right now—it would be the part when I'm sitting at the top of the hill in my bucket, looking out at the other rides and people below me, and waiting in suspense for the frightening descent to begin. The last part would be me sitting white-knuckled in my car as it bumps and lurches around corners, spiraling downwards as I try to hold back tears and hope that I don't fall out and die.

Die.

The sides of my face get hot, and I blink back tears. I take a deep breath. I don't know why it's so hard to say it to Wyndham. I already told Laurence. Although I was furious; it just sort of tumbled out of me accidentally.

Another deep breath, and as I breathe out, I say with my lower lip beginning to tremble again, "Momma has cancer."

"Why do they wish to send you away?"

"So that Mom can have treatment while I'm gone. I

117

overheard them talking one night." My eyes focus again on the dirt. I'm twisting and turning my hands around me, and I continue saying, "And Dad said it will be hard on her. They don't want me to see it. Mom and Dad don't want me to know the truth."

"Your parents wish to protect you?"

"Yes," I say. And then I begin to slurp my words and mumble, "Just like Alwyn. He asked me to stay back from your rescue for the same reason, and now look what's happened to him!" I sob.

"Jayden, Jayden." Wyndham places his hand on my chin and forces my head up, and then he says, "You did not do this. Alwyn did not get hurt because of you. 'Tis a mess."

"'Tis," I say. My eyes go wide. My lower lip drops as my mouth opens.

Oh no. I've done it. I've openly made fun of how Wyndham talks.

I watch as Wyndham begins to shake with laughter.

"Yes, Wyndham does speak in a long-winded way. You could feel the flowers blossom. Ahhhh, perhaps see it happen, with his many words! As children, my brothers and I would tease him about his choice of vocabulary," Constance says as her eyes dart back and forth between me and Wyndham with mischief.

I can't help myself. I laugh even harder.

Constance gives Wyndham a sideways glance with a sideways smile.

After I stop laughing, Constance says, "Your mother is ill?"

"Yeah," I say. I can't believe it. It was hard at first to talk about Mom being sick, but now that I've started, it was definitely getting easier.

"'Tis a lot for a little girl to carry on her own,"

Constance says as she grabs my hands and holds them tightly. But her playful smile is still there.

"'Tis," I say.

"Speak to your parents. Tell them what you know and how you feel. Alwyn is being tended to by our good King's doctors. There are many things I wish I would have told him. There are many things I wish I would have told a good many people, but never could find the words." Constance's eyes drift away from me while she says this, but her eyes focus on me again by the end of the sentence. She let's go of my hand at that moment.

Constance places her hand on Wyndham's arm gently and says, "Thank you, Father, for all that you have done, for my brothers and I. I know it could not have been easy. But you were the only one who would keep us together. You kept us fed, clothed, and built a home for us."

I've never seen this before. Wyndham looks unsettled. I watch as he shifts from foot to foot, places his hands on his hips, and then removes his hands from his sides.

His eyes are moist. Wyndham says, "I did my best. I'm certain there were things I could have done better. Things, I wish I had."

Constance squeezes Wyndham's arms. She leans in and kisses him on the cheek. Her words are broken, and she says, "You did well, Father." Then she turns and walks away.

Me and Wyndham watch as Constance sails away from us. Before she gets too far away, I have to ask her, "How's Alwyn?"

Constance stops, twists around, and raises her eyes to meet mine. "As Wyndham said, all that has passed here is too much for someone so small. But I will not assume, as your parents have, that you cannot bear the truth. The doctors and nurses are tending to Alwyn. They are doing their best to save his life. He is, however, in a perilous state." As she stares at me, she smiles and says, "But hope is not lost." With that, Constance spins around and sweeps through the crowd as she walks towards Eustace and Laurence.

"Like a thief under cover of darkness, she has stolen all the words I wished to say to you." Wyndham stands there with one hand at his side. "You will think all the wisdom I have offered to you through the years came from her."

I laugh and say, "Or the other way around. Mom says the apple doesn't fall far from the tree."

"What is the meaning of this?" Wyndham asks.

"Mom says I take after Dad in some ways," I answer.

I jump off the tree stump. I begin to walk towards Constance, Eustace, and Lawrence as Bob follows me. I wave at Wyndham and yell, "Let's go see what the plan is for getting Enisseny back."

Wyndham nods his head and says, "I now receive my orders from children." He looks around at the trees, the walls of the blue cave, and the flowers that bloom everywhere.

Then he turns, quickly marches past me, and once he's ahead, he waves his hand at me and says, "Let's."

CHAPTER 13

Constance brought me a pair of pants that belonged to Petronilla, as well as a shirt, so I can change clothes. The pants are a little tight at the bottom as I'm taller than Alwyn's daughter. But then Constance cut slits in the cloth around my ankles using a knife, and now they fit better. The shirt is really comfortable.

Laurence leans against the wall of the cave with his arms folded against his chest and shouts, "We must do something! They have Enisseny. Besides, they know that we are here. It will not be long before they attack the cave!"

The King stands back, glances over at Wyndham, and says, "This is the boy you say will be a knight?"

I'm standing off to the side beside Constance. Wyndham is in the center with the other knights and soldiers. We headed to the meeting area and were about to check with the King to see what the plan was to get Enisseny away from Droart and Lord Fulke. But Laurence was a lot less subtle about it. Laurence is right, though, about the other Hunters. They know we're here, and it probably won't take long for them to figure out where we're hiding. I overhear Eustace lean in and say to Constance that we don't have an advantage in the cave. But Osgoode quietly says, "More people are in the cave than those who remain of the Hunters."

"Yes," Wyndham answers as his eyes rest on Laurence.

I don't misbehave very often, but I sometimes do. And Wyndham's "look" is the same as my Dad's. When I misbehave, Dad will stare at me without blinking or smiling, and he'll hold it long enough that I see the white part in his eyes. I don't know what it is about that look, but it settles me down almost immediately. Dad isn't serious very often, but when he is, I better knock off whatever I'm doing because he means business.

Wyndham blinks, takes a big breath in, and says, "His skill with the sword is good. He is fearless, and he has a good, kind soul. But his fearlessness makes him reckless, and he has not yet learned how to control what he says, or whom he says it to. He is a knight in heart, but he lacks the training and guidance to wield the sword without the need for glory."

"I remember my grandfather spoke of another man in much the same manner."

Wyndham blushes and says, "Yes, my King."

"Bring the prisoners here," the King commands.

Two of the knights help the prisoners up. They stand before the King. The King says, "Do you know where Lord Fulke has hidden the dragon?"

The two tower guards' eyes flicker at each other as if they are silently making an agreement. The big guy that it took Toly, Alwyn, Eustace, and Osgoode to carry in says, "We shan't tell you. Yer nut ur King. You've nevr elped us bef're. I av'e already elped yer men, so they dun't fall to their deaths as thee uther."

The King stares at the man and says, "I am here. We have soldiers and knights, and we will protect your people. But we must free Enisseny. If Lord Fulke unleashes Rescol on your people, you will need him."

Eustace told the King about Lord Fulke's threat that he would unleash Rescol on the Hunters when he arrived with his men. The King was furious.

"Why, dat?" the big guy says.

"We will need the dragon's breath to freeze the air in your land. That will stop the spread of the illness. Do not underestimate the power of the White Winter Dragon."

"But we'v jest retrn'd? We've jest gut ur land back? You would ave us lose it again? If the drugun freeze thee ayr, he'll ki'll the soyl and fr'ze the wuter. Wee'll l've us animals withut enuff fud to eat or water to drinke? Besides, a lutta people died in Rambl'n Town, ev'n with thee drugun."

"If the worst were to happen, your people would be welcome to stay on the King's acres. There is plenty of room there, and we would see to it your people would have shelter and food."

The King pauses and then says, "With Rescol and Rumbling Town, Enisseny could only halt the spread of the illness. For those already infected, the fight was within each person's body. Their fate was left to the defenses within themselves."

The man's nose curls up. He spits at the feet of the King. I raise my eyes to Constance, who stands beside me. Her lower lip has dropped open, and her eyes are wide. I don't know what the rules are here, but where I come from, that's not done. Based on Constance's face, I suspect you don't do that to a King here, either.

"Ye lie, my King. Yea did nutt'n to help us those two undred yrs. Why wud ye now?"

"You are mistaken." Osgoode's voice comes through the crowd. "Wyndham has always done his best to help us; he had protected our young when they were caught stealing food for us in nearby villages. I know because it happened to my youngest brother some years ago when we sent him to steal bread from a baker in the town. My brother nearly lost his hand, but Wyndham intervened. Wyndham took the baker to Lord Everard. I was told the baker's punishment for his cruelty towards my brother imposed by the Lord, was to donate a full week's wages to feed my family. That was the reason our family was able to buy food for a short time and shared it with the other Hunters who traveled with us. The first time I met Wyndham was when he delivered the money."

There are gasps throughout the crowd. Constance whisper-mumbles, "We never knew. He never told us."

Wyndham's eyes have drifted away. He's somewhere else right now. Is he back at that moment?

Maybe.

Quietly, I wonder if that was around the time when William came to help us, and it's the story Wyndham told me more than four years ago when I saw him with a cut on his face. Although, Wyndham's gotten hurt so many times since then, it could be any one of those other times.

Wyndham turns and gives a small nod in my direction.

The guard shouts, "Then why wud none share their land with us? Why was Whyndem not able to osk on ur behulf?"

Osgoode's lips are a thin smile. "We assumed past towns we asked were the same as future ones. We waged war on them based on what had already happened. We did not give them the chance to help. We lived the life of warriors. Wyndham tried to convince some townspeople to let us live with them. But none trusted us, and for good reason."

"Besides," Osgoode pauses for a moment, "Wyndham told me that our land was better. That we should travel back and live there. We would not have come back if it weren't for him. However, it did take some time to convince those in command to return."

The guard focuses all his attention on Wyndham. Wyndham doesn't notice. His head's bowed, and he rubs his forehead. For the first time since I've known him, Wyndham seems small and defeated.

"'Tis true?" the prisoner asks.

"Yes." Wyndham's eyes flicker up at the guard. "I asked the King's grandfather after our battle some two hundred years ago if I could watch your people, and do what I could to help. But your people never trusted me, nor Enisseny. We were forced to do all things from afar, and under secrecy. It was only with Osgoode that Enisseny found a special heart. With Osgoode, we could reveal who we were, and from there, build a plan for your people to return to their homes."

"Something special? In me?" Osgoode asks, perplexed.

"Yes," Wyndham says as his eyes drift to the ground before he raises them and they rest on Osgoode. Wyndham scrunches his face and says, "The dragon knows a person's heart. But he cannot see the future. I am sorry, Osgoode." Wyndham's voice cracks a bit, he rubs his temples again as if he has a headache, and then he drops his head for a moment. Finally, Wyndham raises his head and says, "We did not know more than half your people would be lost … that Lord Fulke would be the wielder of death. Enisseny and I thought we were doing what was right."

"What is this?" the King asks. He turns to Eustace for a moment. "You told me of Rescol. How did Lord Fulke kill half the Hunters?"

I say, "Sorry," and shift. I look at Osgoode, Eustace, and the King and begin to cry. "I forgot to tell you about it. Osgoode told me and Laurence about it when he helped us on the cliff."

The King stands there in silence as a soldier would; not one muscle moves, or one strand of hair on his head.

Osgoode's face changes and becomes the same color as Enisseny's coat. For such a tall, strong guy, he walks towards me quietly. When he arrives, he rests a hand on my shoulder and says, "Do not cry, Jayden. There has been much that has happened."

My lower lip trembles. Tears stream down my face. I mumble to him, "I don't want you to think your people don't matter to me. That I forgot because I don't care."

Osgoode bends forward. His face is right in front of me now. I have to look at him. Osgoode says in a whisper to me, "My dear, if I ever thought such a thing, I would be a fool. You care so much for everyone—whether it be family, friends, or strangers. There is much that has happened in a short time. Neither Wyndham nor I told the King either. We have not had the time. Promise me you will do something for me?" he says.

I can't speak, so I nod.

"Be kind to yourself."

I blow bubbles at him through tears. I still can't speak so, I bob my head up and down at him.

Constance arrives and takes my hand in hers. This seems to reassure Osgoode. He places his hand on her elbow, and she gives him a glance that says, *don't worry about her. I've got her.*

Osgoode takes a deep breath in, spins around, and in a deep voice, says, "The Hunters that wished to be farmers were killed when I went to fetch Wyndham."

The King's eyes are focussed on only Osgoode. His hands close and become fists.

Osgoode continues, "Toly said that the farmers would not go along with Lord Fulke's plan to capture the dragon. They were forced into an old barn. Those who agreed to capture the dragon were instructed to set the barn ablaze."

I gently squeeze Constance's hand without meaning to, and when she glances down at me, I notice tears stream down her face.

"Toly said the Warring Hunters did not want to kill their people." Osgoode pauses and continues, "But Lord Fulke threatened to unleash Rescol on them. So, they did as they were told." Osgoode's voice is soft, and in between cracked words, he says, "When I arrived … they showed Wyndham and I the barn. We saw what remained of them. After, they took us to the dungeon." He pauses. One hundred years pass as we wait for him to continue.

Or, so it seems.

I wipe my nose with my sleeve. Everyone has gathered: Laurence in the corner, Eustace, Wyndham, the other knights, and soldiers. It's as if everything is frozen. It's as if we're hoping against all hope that, like in a movie, we'll find out that they're not dead. Or maybe some lived. Some escaped. Perhaps it was all a bad dream. My hands begin to sweat inside of Constance's. I think I'm crying, but I can't really feel anything.

Osgoode says, "They were killed, my King."

"Where is this Toly? We need to speak with him!" the King shouts. "In my land, this has happened!"

Osgoode's head is bent forward; his shoulders are rolled down. He reminds me of Daddy when the world is against him. Then, a low sob comes from where Osgoode is standing.

Oh, no, Toly! I was so distracted with Alwyn, I didn't notice.

I never saw Toly come back!

I pull Constance by the hand in the direction of Osgoode and then let go. Osgoode needs her more than me now. Constance's eyebrows are drooping down. She glances down at me with one of those small gentle smiles. She squeezes my arm once before she heads in the direction of Osgoode.

When Constance arrives, she places her hand on Osgoode's arm. He raises his eyes to her. She quietly takes him by the hand and leads him away, as Wyndham says …

"He has been lost in battle, my King. Protecting his friend's life and saving Alwyn."

Wyndham turns towards the guard and looks him square in the eye.

The guard says, "In frunt uv everyun, my King. You make ye promises to me that ye'll help my people. Yu lie, I'll take ye head, if ye don't do as ye say."

The King's chin is raised and punched out. His eyes are hard. In between clenched teeth and an unbreakable face, the King says, "By my word, if I do not help your people, I will give you my head." He continues, "But if you betray us to Lord Fulke along the way, we will end your life without a second thought to thee."

The guard nods and says, "If I betrey ya, I w'll end mee own lyfe." There's a pause, and he says, "I w'll tell ya wh're the drugun is."

CHAPTER 14

"Are you ready, Jayden?" Laurence asks me.

I glance down as water spins around the moat—the moat that circles the castle where Enisseny is being held.

I take a deep breath in, breathe out, and answer honestly, "Not really."

A whisper of a smile crosses Laurence's face. He grabs my right hand and says, "We will jump together. You will see. This will be easier than climbing Mount Lieuschanean."

"Are you forgetting someone?" Constance's eyes scrunch together in annoyance at Laurence.

Constance never wanted me to do this. She said it was too dangerous.

The guard from the tower (he told us his name was Gamel) said that someone small was needed. But first, we would need to steal some keys from the guards that would open multiple doors. Once we had the keys, the "little person" would then travel along a very narrow and tiny hidden passage to enter the room where Enisseny was being held. Once inside, the keys would unlock the door and the chains that held Enisseny. To open the door above Enisseny, (it's the only way the dragon can leave the room) requires the strength of at least two men to turn a wheel that would swing the door open above the dragon.

Droart apparently put the system in place so that it would always take more than one person to release the dragon, and also a short person to enter the room. (Him, primarily; but because I'm small, I work, too.)

One of the knights asked, *With all of Enisseny's powers, how can he not free himself?*

Wyndham spat the words at the other knight and answered, *They are chains! Enisseny has powers, but he can still be bound by the same things that will hold any other man or beast!*

Thee drugen, he did tre, Gamel continued. His eyes flickered at Wyndham before he said, *He did speel h's blud whon he tre to break thee chins. He cud not. If the drugun did not stup, the wizard, he cast a speel, make the drugun beheeve. Make thee drugun quiet.*

I've never seen Wyndham lose it before. His exact words were these: *Oh, Mother of Canonsland, and great god! Wyndham threw his hands up in frustration and shouted, DROART IS NO WIZARD! He is a man that does well in mixing different herbs together—that which may be found in trees, flowers, and in the ground! Indeed, some powers cannot be explained. But do not be so quick as to think it is that of wizardry. Turn to your knowledge of things that may offer some explanation, exhaust all other possibilities, and if you cannot find the answer, you may turn to the realm of magic and myth.*

The short answer is this: Enisseny was drugged.

When I was at school one day last year, a black bear came around. He pushed over the garbage can, and when he was done eating whatever was in it, he wandered over and started to tug on the swings on our playground. Ms. Song couldn't help but smile too, as she told us we couldn't go outside for our afternoon break. We watched out the window and waited for the Park Rangers to arrive. Once they arrived, they shot it. I was scared when I saw the bear get hit, and then he slowly slumped down. But Ms. Song said, *The Rangers just tranquilized it, so they can move it back to the woods.*

Although, the drug Droart used, would have been both a tranquilizer and something that messed with Enisseny's mind. Enisseny flew himself and Droart into the castle, where he is now imprisoned.

The reason I'm part of Enisseny's Rescue Operation is because I'm small, just like Droart. The passage is very narrow, and a full-grown man or woman wouldn't fit through it.

No pressure. It's up to me to free the dragon. The King, Wyndham, Eustace, Osgoode, the knights, and the soldiers will be going through the front. While everyone is distracted with the people at the front door, we'll be swimming in the slightly stinky moat water that I'm looking down at right now, climb our way through a drainage vent, (double yuck) and then make our way up some stairs that will take us to the top of the castle. Gamel told us, *Take thee stairs to thee tup. There ye shull fund the drugun.*

The King released Gamel. He's on our side now and fights with everyone at the front door. Some soldiers stayed back in the Garden Cave to protect the doctors, nurses, Alwyn, and some of the other injured people. Gamel's friend was less eager to help, so he's still tied up. The soldiers are keeping an eye on him, too.

Wyndham, at first, didn't want me to be a part of Enisseny's rescue. Gamel suggested he might be able to convince one of the children in his city, Ikansterup, to do it. But I told Wyndham that I could do it and that we didn't have time to find someone else. Wyndham started to make a bunch of excuses why I shouldn't go, and I said to him, *What does it say if we send one of the Hunters' children in, but not me? Does it mean my life's more valuable than their children's?* Wyndham just stood above me, stepped back, folded his arms together in front of him, and a few seconds later said, *You are wise beyond your years, Jayden.*

Gamel's this big burly guy who's quite round, with a thick, long black beard, and his eye color almost looks black, too. When he heard me say that, he just stared at me for a few moments with a look. It's hard to describe, really. I remember his eyebrows were pulled forward a bit, and these thick lines appeared out of nowhere, and his mouth was open a bit. I saw him lift his hand and rub his eye. There are all kinds of crazy scents in the Garden Cave, so there was something that was probably bothering him.

I have allergies, too. I get it.

Gamel loves his people. He just wants to protect them and help them. I think we convinced him that what we said was true and that we'll help them this time. We promised him.

When the plan had been finalized, Wyndham told Osgoode and Constance about it. Constance flipped out a bit when she found out I was a crucial player in the rescue. Constance said, *How could you, Wyndham? She is a small girl. Who will protect her? There will be men wielding swords! The Hunters do not know that we will help them be free of Lord Fulke. They may hurt her.*

Then there were lots of words being thrown around back and forth between Wyndham and Constance. In the end, she decided she was coming to take care of me. Oddly enough, it doesn't bother me. I like Constance— she looks out for me. Laurence tried to object to his big sister coming, but Wyndham stopped him. Wyndham told everyone that Constance studied with him on swordsmanship for the last ten years and was quite good. Wyndham said, *Constance fights with the same strength as ten men. Do not assume because she bakes, she cannot defend herself or those she loves.*

Me and Wyndham talked about it afterward, when no one else was around. He told me, *She is better with the sword than Laurence.* Then Wyndham raised one eyebrow at me and said, *Do not tell Laurence. He is an arrogant young man and would be unsettled to learn his older sister is better than him.* Wyndham's arms were folded in front of him, and he quietly chuckled, raised one eyebrow, and whispered to me, *I wish to tell Laurence when the time is right.*

When Wyndham told everyone about Constance being able to use a sword, it was quite funny. All the men were horrified, but most of all, Laurence. The only exceptions were Eustace, and I'm not sure, but possibly also Osgoode. Osgoode didn't say anything. He just stood there with a small smile on his face and a crinkle in his nose, and his eyes twinkled at Constance.

I'm glad Wyndham taught Constance how to protect herself. After all, she has three brothers, and Wyndham could have decided that they should take care of her. But he didn't. Maybe he realized that she might need to protect herself in case they weren't around.

Wyndham's too cool. He may be old, but he thinks women can do anything that men can do. I love that about him.

Bob stayed back in the Garden Cave. The King brought with him doctors and nurses who could take care of anyone who got hurt along the way, or if a battle happened, they would help heal the injured—on both sides. I gave Bob strict instructions to take care of Alwyn.

He snuggled close to Alwyn's leg at the end of his bed. Both of them were asleep when we left. But Bob popped his head up for a minute when I turned around to see him one last time and then plopped his head back down against Alwyn's foot.

I said, *Good dog.*

The narrow passage thing bothers me a lot. I wonder if now might be a good time to mention to Laurence that I get nervous in small spaces?

I decide it's probably too late. Instead, I grab Laurence's hand in my left, and Constance's in my right. We all look up, and I think I see a group of men riding horses. I hear the faint sounds of hoofs that clip-clop along the dusty road, and they throw dust into the air, making it difficult to see what's happening. (The King's men went back for the horses after they found out about the safe route through the cave.)

Then, there is the low, baritone, ominous sound of the King's horn being blown. This would be the announcement that the King, the knight Edric, Wyndham, Osgoode, Eustace, and Gamel want to speak with the people in the castle.

Wyndham said, *We will avoid bloodshed if we can.*
But the horn is also our signal to jump.

My heart thumps in my chest. Then me, Laurence, and Constance step backward a few steps. Our hands are clasped together. Slippery sweat makes it difficult to hang onto one another. We slowly move our legs from a walk to a jog and then transition to a run as we hurtle ourselves forward and leap from the edge into the black liquid that surrounds the castle. The darkness swallows each one of us. But despite the sweat, our running, and the jumping, we never let go of the hands we hold.

Together, we descend into darkness.

***

"Jayden, Jayden!" Laurence's voice is the first I hear when I surface. I choke on water, and both Constance and Laurence hold me up.

"Can you swim?" Laurence whispers to me.

I frown at him, push myself backward, and begin doing the butterfly stroke that I learned in swim class. After a few seconds, I turn my head back to Laurence. I watch his head bob in the water like one of those bobbly heads on cars and shout, "Of course, I can swim!"

Constance's face lights up, she begins giggling, and then she swims over to me and says, "Shhh … We must be quiet now. There will be guards scattered in the castle. We do not know where they will be. It will be best if we speak in hushed tones."

"Oh," I say. "Okay. Sorry. Never been a part of a rescue operation before."

Constance's hair is caked against her face, and she pushes it back with her hand. Her arms move up and down in the popular swim style of the doggie paddle. Constance's head bobs up and down as she giggles a bit, occasionally spitting water out here and there, and says, "Neither have I."

"Follow me," Laurence whispers as he takes long breaststrokes past me and Constance.

I watch Constance roll her eyes as Laurence passes us. I do the same. We both shake our heads and follow him. I'm the very last person on our team.

When we get to the wall of the castle, Laurence finds the vent where there is an opening. But we have to hold our breath and dive down a little, then swim back up, and go through the opening. Laurence enters first to see if it's clear. He returns a few minutes later, spraying water at us like whales do from their blowholes when they surface.

"The way is clear. But we must hold our breath for several minutes," he announces when he returns. Laurence turns to me and Constance and says, "Will there be any difficulty?"

Constance says, "Not for me, Laurence. Jayden?"

"I don't think so," I say. "But I've never had to hold my breath that long before."

Constance says, "You go first, Laurence. That way, if there is any trouble, you can tend to it for us. Wyndham says you are good with the sword."

I smile at Constance. I wonder if she knows what Wyndham said about her. With her flattering words, I watch Laurence's chest balloon out again, and he says, "I have studied, Sister."

Constance's lips are tight, and she's suddenly serious, and says, "I know."

Constance glances at me and says, "You will be second, Jayden. If you have any difficulties, do not worry. I will be behind you to help."

With that, we all take a deep breath, dive under the water, and I keep my eyes open as instructed by Laurence so that I can see where I'm going. (The water really isn't that dirty.) I follow Laurence through the opening and turn a moment to look for Constance. I'm relieved when I see she's right behind me.

Laurence is quite a ways ahead of me now. Constance grabs my hand, and we swim together.

Laurence's body suddenly stops in the water. I move my hands faster as I get more desperate for air. A second later, I gulp water. It burns through my throat. My eyes go wide as I struggle to breathe. Then, a hand pulls me towards her, and I wrap one arm around her neck. Water swirls around us. In between blinks, I see Constance kick faster with her legs as she digs deep into the water with one hand, so we go further while holding onto me with the other arm.

A hand reaches towards Constance, and she grabs it. We break the surface of the water. I heave in air while simultaneously spitting water in all directions. My throat burns as if it's on fire.

Constance beams at me. Then, I lean over her shoulder and spit water out. She rubs my back and says, "You did well, Jayden."

I begin to cough as quietly as I can. I remember what Constance said. We have to be quiet now.

The guards can be anywhere.

CHAPTER 15

Jayden, Constance, and Laurence slowly make their way through the castle. At the front of the stone gates that lead to the city, the King, Edric, Wyndham, Eustace, Osgoode, and Gamel wait to see what Lord Fulke's next move will be. It's during this time of inaction that Eustace's mind reflects on many things.

The pouring of sweat is felt down the side of my face and gathers in the whiskers of my beard because of the blazing sun above us. My riding gloves slide back and forth through the horse's reins, as we wait for what will befall us next.

Gamel's head turns to me, and he says, "Ya good, with thee suard?"

I lie to him and say, "I am not as good as Wyndham, nor Laurence, but I can fight if I must." The truth be told, I am better with words than with weapons. I prefer to leave the fighting to Wyndham and Laurence, and deal with people through rational thought. I am always thinking, considering my next steps.

I lied to Gamel because I do not trust him. I fear that if we are in battle, he will make a quick end to me if the time is right, and he knows my weakness. I do not know if he believes all that we said when we promised to help his people. He may think we only care for the release of Enisseny.

I cannot blame him for not trusting us. We did nothing to help his people for hundreds of years. Now that he sits on a horse beside me, I see our neglect up close: His beard has not been trimmed in the manner it should: his clothes are faded, and sewn patches cover his garments; his eyes show his weariness. Osgoode's manner of dress and his eyes are similar to that of Gamel's.

Osgoode is an interesting fellow. He is visibly a robust man, who also has an incredible level of tenderness, rarely seen in a man such as him. After all that has happened to him … all that he has lost … I wonder if he will find happiness again in this life?

While in the presence of Constance, Osgoode is shy and uncomfortable as he shifts about on his feet, while doing his best to put words together. It is odd because, when she is not in the same room as him, he is very good at getting his thoughts in order. Constance, for her part, like with everyone, is good at quieting Osgoode and bringing calmness to his world, even in grief.

But for my only sister, I see something new in her as well. She is both shy and bold when she is with him and speaks with a tenderness in her voice that I have not heard before.

Perhaps, even with all that Osgoode has lost, they can find happiness together.

Now that I have seen several of the Hunters, I have no doubt they have suffered. How could so many of us in Canonsland be so blind? The Hunters were starving, poorly clothed, and we gave them nothing.

My family and I do not have much, but Wyndham has always seen to it that the most basic of our needs have been met. Thanks to Lord Everard, who gave Wyndham the decaying castle, we were given shelter as children. But it was Wyndham who did his best to repair the building, while also providing food for us that turned the dilapidated building into a home. Our Father did all this while tending to his other duties as a knight. Now Wyndham has given the land and the castle to me, Alwyn, Constance, and Laurence to share. It is ours, he has said.

But the Hunters did not have that. For certain, some Hunters are now adults who have never known the comforts of an orange-red fire in a hearth, and warm food on a table, where brothers, sisters, and parents would gather to share a meal—for they were forced to walk this land with no shelter above them.

I do not make eye contact with Gamel. I turn my attention to the doors that lie before us for the smallest of moments. Then, I quickly glance to the right and left of the doors. I look to see if anyone is laying in wait for us. Above us, I notice guards that stand on the walkway of the castle planks. As well, off to the side of the castle, there are two men whose heads poke out for the briefest of moments, only to return to their not-so-secret hiding post behind green yangling shrubs.

Wyndham's eyes peer over at me, and he says in a quiet voice, "Eustace, what do you see?"

I look blankly far off to the side, where I have not seen anyone hiding. My hope is to keep my thoughts to myself, lest my eyes give away what I have noticed.

The Hunters surround us.

Albeit, there is a good chance that the Hunters, too, know we are hiding men. We are six men that stand before them, one of which is the King. Lord Fulke and the Hunters would expect that the King's soldiers are close by, waiting to charge forward to protect their sovereign.

My eyes are cast this way and that way, as I say, "There are men on the planks that link the castle together, and men who hide in the bushes."

Wyndham smiles and says, "Yes, indeed. They are but a few."

My lips tighten wearily, and I add, "There are heads that I see to the left. They are hidden in the darkness of the castle walls behind the gates. I cannot make out how many, but I would say at least ten men are there, if not more."

Wyndham places his left hand on his leg, smiles, and says, "'Tis the reason I brought you. You are good at seeing things that I will sometimes miss. You also possess the skill to speak with people and cool tempers that flare. With you, I hope to avoid further bloodshed."

With these words, the gates are thrust open, and one man charges towards us on horseback. The knight named Edric, who held Jayden back when Alwyn returned to the Garden Cave, is the first to swing his sword out. He rides forward and places himself in front of the King. Wyndham's lips straighten for a moment when he looks over at Edric. Then he turns, and gallops towards the unknown Hunter.

Wyndham's sword remains tucked in his belt. I race after him with my weapon in its place, as my father has done. I hear distant hoofs behind me and look over my shoulder to see it is Osgoode.

The King, the knight Edric, and Gamel are swiftly following behind us. I see that Edric has returned his sword to its place.

We face a red-haired Hunter with dark eyes and dark skin. His face is contorted in a twisted sea of emotions that screams across his face. Wyndham has given us strict instructions not to mention Enisseny unless asked.

Our purpose, as we are to say, is this: We are here to deal with that which happened to the farmers amongst the Hunters. That is the reason the King has come. It is a truth. The King has made it very clear that Lord Fulke will pay for all that he has done. Unlike the unleashing of Rescol that killed our parents, where there was no evidence of the deed, this time, Lord Fulke has left a scattered trail of twisted grief for many people. This is easily pointed in the direction of him. Lord Fulke will receive his comeuppance.

But Enisseny will be rescued, as well.

"Are you the knight, Wyndham?" the man asks with a head that twists around and eyes that skip among all of us as if he's doing his best to figure it out. He says the words in a spirit that is broken.

"Yes," Wyndham answers. His voice and eyes belong to only the Hunter who stands before him now.

The Hunter's lined face shows his age, similar to the rings that form inside a tree revealing how long it's lived. The red-haired man glances past Wyndham and says, "Is that you, Gamel? And Osgoode?"

Both answer, "Yes."

The man turns towards Wyndham and says, as his voice crunches like snow beneath one's feet, "Do you know what has happened?"

Wyndham moves towards the man, closing the gap between them, and says, "I know all that has transpired here."

Those are the red-haired man's last words.

Osgoode's voice roars in my ear, "ARROW!!!!"

We turn, and we see arrows fly from the castle walls towards us! We scatter in all directions! Then, the gates open to the left, where I saw men hiding. Hunters rush towards us with raised swords! I watch Wyndham jump from his horse towards the red-haired man, knocking him from his steed. Behind us, the King's men storm forward with shouts, raised swords, and the quick speed of feet turning over. Some of the soldiers and knights are on stallions, some on foot. I search for Wyndham and see that he has drawn his sword. The red-haired man pulls his! With that, I release my weapon from my belt and stand ready to fight.

The battle has commenced!

***

The castle is damp, and water droplets drip from the ceiling and along the walls causing puddles to form in certain areas on the floor. It's a good thing because we didn't bring a change of clothes, and honestly, even if we'd carried them in a bag, there was no way we could have kept them dry while we swam. Constance says, *We did not plan on that part of it. The water that falls from our drenched clothes might have given us away. So the ruination of the castle works in our favor.*

We're hiding behind a pillar in the castle; Laurence is behind one, and me and Constance peek out from behind another. In front of us are about ten Hunters. One of them throws his hands up and says, "They're alone! Six of 'em! Let's watch 'em get slaughtered!"

Immediately, Constance sprints from our pillar to Laurence's. She grabs Laurence by the elbow and places her hand on top of his, as he begins to reach for his sword. Constance glares at him for a moment and then points to a stairwell behind him.

So far, Gamel was right about everything he told us. Gamel helped in the preparations of the room where the dragon would be kept, and that's why he knows the layout of the castle so well. He said Lord Fulke trusted

143

him the most, probably because he was the angriest of all the Hunters. Not in those exact words, but that's the short version.

Constance glances at the men who are standing at the window as they continue to cheer. Then, she sweeps her hand towards herself, gesturing for me to come over. Blood rushes through me, and without hesitating, I sprint towards Laurence and Constance and squeeze in as close as I can to them. Once there, Constance points in the direction of the stairs. All of us are on tiptoes as we ascend the stairs, in hopes we will find Enisseny.

We climb and climb the narrow staircase. But, as we continue our ascent, my breathing becomes louder as the endless staircase goes on and on. I begin to worry I might alert some guards that we don't see. From behind me, I hear a quiet, "Huhuhuhu …" sound. I peer over my shoulder, and notice Constance is struggling to keep her breathing quiet as well. I stare at Laurence's back in front of me, as he continues to sprint up the stairs. I can barely hear anything from him. He's like a cat. You don't know he's there until it's too late. My fists become balled, and I clench my jaw without meaning to. I hate to say it, but I'm a little jealous he can climb stairs better than us.

We hear something. It's the sound of chains scraping along the floor above us. Constance places her hand over my chest to stop me, and I notice that Laurence has stopped as well. When I look over at Constance, her eyes are glassy like the mirror in my bedroom.

Enisseny has not been captured in a long time. Constance's face reminds me of the story that Wyndham told me: How the people of Rumbling Town were always the ones to save and release Enisseny when he was caught. But, the people never asked anything of Enisseny in return for their kindness. I suspect Enisseny stopped to help the people of Rumbling Town all those years ago when they were attacked by the Hunters because the town always took care of him.

Today, the people of Rumbling Town are helping him again.

But this time, the rescuers also include me, and some of the Hunters.

When we arrive at the top, there's a long hallway, and we see some guards who stand in front of a black wooden door. Laurence pokes his head around the corner, and five fingers pop up, signaling five guards. Constance touches her sword, and Laurence nods.

Purr-breathing is all I hear.

Enisseny.

There's a *clink-clink* and then a *chhhhh*. It sounds like Enisseny is shifting behind the door.

My eyes are swallowed up with tears. Poor Enisseny! Desperate, I frantically crane my neck around corners in search of the keys. After some time, I still can't find them. Annoyed, I blink at Laurence and Constance. They appear to be arguing in sign language (sort of), but I have not a clue about what.

I have a responsibility here for the first time ever. I can't fail!

I need to find those keys, go down the small and claustrophobic hidden passage, unlock the doors from the inside, and then we will all work to open the door above Enisseny, and we can fly out on him.

My eyes see something.

THE KEYS!!! I grin, exuberantly at them.

There's only one problem, though. The keys are off to the right side of the wall that's beside Enisseny's door. But the wall is in full view of the guards. There's no way I can get to them.

With a huff, I breathe out and shift in my spot as I try

to figure out how best to get to the keys.

My head swivels towards Laurence and Constance. They continue their frantic gestures at each other. Occasionally, they will tap each other, and either Constance or Laurence's head will shake from left to right. I don't have siblings, but this must be what it's like when they argue.

A second later, I brighten up. A plan is unfolding in my mind. There's something about grown-ups: Most of the time, adults think kids don't know anything and aren't seen as threatening. I fooled the last guys. I'm pretty confident I can fool these guys.

I run in front of the guards and shout, "Hiya!" And add in a squealing giggle.

A very short soldier, who's wearing a patched-up plaid shirt that droops down over his hands, and pants that when he walks two steps slide down and he has to pull them up, sees me and says, "Henry, did ye hear thut?"

The man, I can only assume is Henry, stops dead. His face becomes white, and he says, "'Tis a ghost."

One of the other guards whispers to no one, "'Tis, a child. This place is haunted!" And he throws his hands up and races down the stairs.

Constance and Laurence are spinning around in circles, as they scan the whole area around Enisseny's prison. Their eyes are wide open, as they frantically continue their search while doing their best not to be seen.

Are they searching for me?

I don't understand. Can no one see me?

I walk behind Mr. Baggy Pants and tap him on the shoulder and yell, "BOO!" into his ear.

His hand flies in my direction, but I duck his hand-swat move. I stick one finger out and jab him in the side of his ribs. He throws his weapon on the floor, screams, "AHH!!! 'TIS A GHOST!" and races down the stairs.

I'm smiling as I watch him leave.

Who says kids can't do stuff?

Suddenly, arms are wrapped tightly around me. I swing my head up and look at the guard.

The guard, Henry, says, "That is an interesting trick, child, but I have you now!"

Laurence charges forward with his sword out, and right behind him is Constance in the same way. The guard throws me aside, and now all three of the guards have their swords drawn.

I hear the ringing sound of metal clashing together as both Laurence and Constance begin a swordfight with the three guards. Then thumping feet are on the stone stairs with someone asking, "Whut's appn'd?" question.

I'm torn as I look at what's going on. *I have two choices.* I can run and grab the keys and start my way down the narrow passage. I think I see a lever on the floor. Or, before I do that, there's another door that I can close. It would prevent more guards from joining the fight against Laurence and Constance.

I run towards the door as fast as I can and swing it shut. I step up on a stone ledge to reach the deadbolt lock and flick it over. With that, I jump down and run towards the keys. One of the two guards that Constance fights turns in my direction and races towards me with one arm outstretched and says, "You will not get the keys!"

My feet fly underneath me, and then I am against the wall with the keys. But I'm too short, and I begin to hop up and down, trying to grab them. The guard slows down and starts laughing.

I look over, and Laurence is now fighting two of the guards.

From behind Mr. Chuckles, Constance charges forward at him with an "AAAAAA!" The man pulls his sword out, just as Constance's sword swings up and nicks him on the face. Constance and the guard begin their battle again. I look hopelessly up at the keys.

I stare up at the keys for a moment, wishing that I was taller. Sure, I closed the door, but I'm still too small to reach the keys. My eyes fill up with tears, and I close them, wishing I was a different person.

Braver. Taller. Smarter.

I blink my eyes open at a memory. *Something that I saw...*

Over to the right, there's a small rotten wooden table with stick legs. I rush over, turn the table over, and tug at the legs as hard as I can. When they don't come out, in frustration, I throw the table against the wall by the leg, and it breaks off.

I stand in front of the keys with my stick, reach up, and use it to drag the keys along the holder until they fall to the ground with a *clunk!*

"YES!" I squeal.

I grab the keys and push a lever that is located at ground level. The wall of the castle turns, and I run to the other side.

I poke my head back out for a moment, and I catch Constance's eye. She smiles proudly at me while she continues to fight. The guard follows Constance's gaze and glances down at the keys I hold. He gives a few smacks of his sword in Constance's direction and screams, "NOOOO!!!" before he leaves her and charges in my direction.

With that, I hit the lever on the other side, and the wall turns around and closes me off from everyone and everything. On the ground, where the gear is located, it looks like there is a lock that locks with a key. I grab the keyring and flick through a couple of the keys and find the one with a similar cut. (It's a good thing my dad's in construction.) I stick it in, and it's followed by a clicking sound.

"No, turning back now," I mumble.

I spin around. In front of me is a slightly elevated, square entrance to a narrow dark tunnel. One hop, and I'm on my knees at the stone mouth of the tunnel.

I take another deep breath. My hands are placed at my sides, while my knees scrape along the stone as I crawl through the tunnel that's cold and dark and smells like decomposing food.

My hope: This is the tunnel that leads me to Enisseny.

CHAPTER 16

I can't see anything. I wiggle myself like a worm along the narrow passageway. There isn't even enough room to stand. Worse yet, every now and then, something will run across my fingers, and I yelp almost like I've touched a hot stove. I'm aware that I don't want anyone to know what I'm up to (releasing the dragon), so I turn the yelp into a slight hum. There seems to be something in my hair, and I fling it in an attempt to shoo it out. I'm not sure, but I think it's gone.

Spiders and earwigs are the first things that come to mind. I really hate earwigs because they're gross, and they look slimy, even though they have a crunchy shell. Remembering where I am, it occurs to me if they have earwigs here, they could be the size of Enisseny, and they could devour me in one gulp.

I start to shake a little, thinking about the enormous human-devouring earwig that I created in my mind. I decide my thoughts aren't helping. I've completely stopped moving. My hands are frozen in front of me for only another second, and then I begin crawling again with my right arm and leg synchronized together, and then my left arm and leg. I just got to keep crawling. Don't stop for anything; keep pushing one knee forward.

I think about the positives. It's so dark in the tunnel that I can't see anything, and I have no idea how terrible the insects or mice might look, or how large they really are.

That might not be much of a positive.

I decide to think about my quest—to release Enisseny!

As I slowly inch my way along in the darkness, I'm relieved when I see the light again that pokes through at the end of the stone tunnel I've been moving along. I am elated and want to let out a *Whoop!* That would be followed by the question: *Who knew it would be so easy?* I thought there would be another door that would be locked. But maybe Droart figured he made it difficult enough and that there was no reason to add another security level at the very end.

My relief lasts only a few seconds. I arch my head forward to hear better, and it's a man's voice, but I can't identify him. I relax my breathing so that way I'm not detected, and also so I can hear what's being said.

"HAHA! They will lose! You will see! The guards will end them, and your knight will say good-night for the final time as well!" His voice is scratchy like a cat's meow. I hear feet that *tap, tap, tap* on the floor. It sounds like he's dancing. My lips close, and I scowl at him from inside my tunnel. I would kick him right now if he were in front of me.

I'm starting to see why Laurence charges into situations all the time, waving his sword. It's tough not to do when you're mad, and it must be twice as hard if you think you're stronger than everyone else.

Inching my way along further, I hear through the door a continuous clinking sound of swords clashing together.

I assume it's most likely Laurence and Constance that are having a marathon swordfight session with the guards.

I hold onto the key tightly because it hangs from a big ring that's sort of like a massive key chain. My hands are sweaty, and I'm trying not to drop the key, so the noise doesn't attract Droart's attention. I know Wyndham said Droart's not a wizard. But he can still give me Rescol. I really don't like being sick—or, for that matter, particularly enjoy the thought of dying.

I crawl closer and stick one eye out through an opening from the tunnel.

"It's a good thing you're drugged, my little dragon!" Droart cackles in the direction of Enisseny. "I would worry about you escaping with your friends so close, but I guess the last dosage you received was enough."

He pauses and says, "Then again, perhaps I should not take any chances."

Suddenly, Enisseny's white tail pops into the tunnel right in front of me. Enisseny keeps his head down, turning it very slowly in my direction. I poke out of the tunnel and see that Enisseny is chained. His head slowly swivels in my direction. His body blocks Droart from seeing me.

Enisseny then gives me a wink-blink.

The dragon's not drugged! He's just pretending!

Enisseny uses his tail to block me from Droart's view. I hide behind his serpent-like tail, as I gently jump down from the tunnel, making sure the key I hold doesn't make a sound. Right now, it can't make so much as a *ding* because Droart and I are in the same room together, and all the people I depend on, Constance and Laurence, are on the other side of the locked door, fighting their own battle.

Enisseny's tail wraps me up, and I follow it to a ledge

that's raised a little, where there's a lock that connects Enisseny's chains. I'm relatively confident if I jump, I might be able to make it to the ledge to unlock him.

"This will be Droart's World …

Droart's World.

The name of Canonsland will be no more …

No More.

No Kings or Lords or Knights.

It will be the wizard's world,

Thee wizard named Droart!

That rules with spells and might!"

I scowl at the sound of his voice. I turn my head to look at the crazy wizard who can't rhyme and who has no rhythm. Droart's head pops up. Our eyes meet.

In less than a second, Enisseny scoops me up on his head and lifts me to the ledge where the lock is to the chains that tie him down. I wiggle the key into the lock and triumphantly squeal out, "Yes!" when they crash to the floor.

Enisseny turns his attention to Droart, who wobbles in a slow run in the direction of a bag, sitting a little ways away on the prison floor. Enisseny's chest expands, his eyes turn red, and he blows white freezing air in the direction of Droart.

Droart freezes in his place.

"Jayden! If you are done in there, we could use Enisseny's help here!" I hear Laurence's sarcastic voice through the door.

"Oh, yeah!" I shout. I stick the key in the lock and unlock the door. But there's also a big tree trunk that barricades the door and stops me from opening it. No matter how much I pull and tug on it, it won't move.

In one swoop, I watch Enisseny grab the tree trunk in his teeth. He heaves it up from across the door and tosses it aside. With a *Whomp!* Enisseny pushes the big doors open, and in front of him stands the three guards, Laurence and Constance. They are all covered in sweat, and are pale, because of their never-ending sword fight.

Laurence and Constance take a few steps back from the men. Laurence says, "Choose now, whether ye wish to join us or not? We know of Lord Fulke and the threat he made to unleash Rescol on your people with the help of the wizard, Droart.

Laurence swings his head out past Enisseny, searching for something. Using the pointy end of his sword, he says, "As you can see, the wizard is no longer a threat. Together, we can beat Lord Fulke."

The man named Henry gazes in the direction where Laurence is pointing. He turns his head away for a moment and rubs his nose for a second. When he turns back, he has tears in his eyes; he nods and says, "We are indebted to you. We will join you."

Laurence nods in agreement, and everyone lowers their swords.

With that, Henry walks over to Droart, and with one swift stroke, he swings his sword up in the direction of the frozen man. Droart splinters into a thousand pieces. Scattered across the floor like a puzzle, the icy remains of the man lie.

Henry grabs the bag that belonged to Droart and passes it to Laurence, saying, "Whatever magic Droart carried in this bag, see to it that it is destroyed. No other people should have to suffer the way the people of Rumbling Town did so many years ago. Or for that matter, our people, who were threatened by it."

Laurence's exhausted face nods at Henry.

Laurence holds the bag and says, "We must open the doors above Enisseny."

Henry walks over and starts to turn a huge wrench. The other men join in, as well as Constance. Laurence turns to me and says, "Jayden, get on the back of Enisseny."

Enisseny gives me a little boost with his nose, and I am now seated on his back. When I'm on top, Laurence hands me the bag and says, "Take care of this." He then runs over and helps with opening the door.

Enisseny has begun to pace a little, as his white tail swishes back and forth, and I can feel his heart beating in his body. I sway from side to side with his movement, but I hang on to his coat to stop me from tumbling off.

In a few seconds, the doors above Enisseny are open.

Laurence says to Henry, "We must go. We must stop any further bloodshed. You can fly with us on Enisseny."

Henry steps back and says, "I do not think so. My feet were meant to walk or run, not to dangle in the heavens. As I make my way to the front of the castle by the stairs, I can tell those who remain what has happened."

The other two guards back away from the white dragon as well.

Constance jumps up and is seated in front of me.

Laurence says, "Alright. But you do not know what you are missing. The view is spectacular."

Henry laughs and says, "I can see breathtaking views from our mountain. I need not spend my time in the heavens until my time is ended here in Canonsland. Thanks to you, I have time left before I depart for another world."

With that, Laurence jumps up behind me on Enisseny. I am, as usual, sandwiched between Laurence and Constance. This time, Constance is first, though, and that thought makes me grin.

As if Enisseny understood every word that has been

said, he begins to flap his wings. We slowly rise from the floor of what was Enisseny's prison until we clear the door above us.

Once we are above the door, Enisseny stretches his neck out, and when he turns his head to the right, I notice his eyes are red. He lets out a window-shattering screech that makes the air quake, buildings below us sway, and even though we're high above it, I'm sure the ground is vibrating.

We continue to roar to the battlefield with what might be the same speed as a shuttle when it is launched into outer space in my world. My eyes are big and expanding every second while my heart thumps as loudly as Enisseny's wings. I hang on tightly to Constance with one hand, while clutching the bag that Laurence has trusted me to keep with the other, all while Enisseny thunders towards the battle below us.

CHAPTER 17

My sword crashes into one of the Hunters who charged at us. One by one, they fall, with losses, felt on our side as well. My hands shake, and sweat pours from my forehead. The sun is unrelenting in its heat during this battle. I am weary. When I think I have a moment, I take a breath in, lean forward, and wipe sweat from my brow.

In front of me, I see Gamel rushing forward. I expected it. Nonetheless, I am shaken from the battle, the lives I have taken, and now this—to have my worst fear realized—to be betrayed by a man that I wished to help!

I ready my sword. But then it fumbles between my fingers. In a moment, I am unarmed. I make my peace, bow my head, and prepare to cross over into another land.

In front of me, I hear, "Do nut arm 'em!"

I raise my head in time for Gamel to shove me to the side. He charges forward, knocking a man to the ground and knocking the sword from his hand. Gamel gives him a good blow on the head, and the man is down.

"I thu, yu sud yu wus gud!" Gamel shouts. His arms and eyebrows are raised at the same time in a fit of exasperation.

My breath comes in short bursts, and I say, "Never … did I say such a thing."

I scurry over and reach for my sword. Before I can clasp my fingers around it, the ground beneath my feet begins to sway. From the heavens, I hear a hawkish screech. There is also the sound of beating drums. The two sounds work against each other.

Everything moves. Everything rattles. The men on both sides are dropping their swords to cover their ears, myself included. Through the sun, I see a white cloud that swarms towards us. I reach desperately for my sword and finally clasp my hands tightly around it. I am terrified to think of what creature Droart may have created.

"Enisseny!!!!!" Wyndham shouts in jubilation.

The deafening sound softens a little, and we gather around Wyndham.

"Have you gone mad, Wyndham?" the King asks. "That is not your dragon."

Wyndham erupts in one of his Wyndham laughs. We wait for an answer. When Wyndham has gotten hold of his emotions, he answers calmly, "I am certain 'tis."

"I have never seen him like that," the King says.

"No," Wyndham answers. When we cannot bear it much longer, he finally continues and says, "Not in your lifetime. It has been over two hundred years since Enisseny took that form."

As the dragon approaches, the reverberating pounding of his wings softens. Then, the wind flutters through his wings, and the beating of drums ends when Enisseny sees we have lowered our swords.

Now the dragon is above us; I see he carries Constance, Laurence, and Jayden. I breathe out a sigh of relief to see the safe return of my brother, sister, and

Jayden. I had not realized I was so worried until this moment.

Laurence jumps from the dragon before he has fully landed. He runs towards Wyndham with his usual energy. Laurence announces under labored breath, "The wizard is dead ... if you have not heard—"

Wyndham turns to him and says, "We had not."

"There was a guard, Henry, I believe, was his name. He was going to tell those in the castle, on his way down to the battle, they no longer need to fear Droart," Laurence continues while bending forward to calm his breathing.

Right at that moment, from behind me, a group of people flow from the castle. Leading the people through the gates is a tall man with broad shoulders who has the mannerisms and physique of a guard. The man leads with such confidence and determination to where we are gathered around the dragon, I can only presume this to be the man, Henry.

I turn my attention back to the dragon. My darling sister may know how to handle a sword in battle, but she has a beautiful mothering quality to her, as well. I watch in admiration as she cares for Jayden, lending a hand to help her down from the dragon. Of course, Osgoode has arrived to help with the task, as well. It does not surprise me that Laurence abandoned them. It does not surprise me that Osgoode helps.

In the child's hands, I notice she is holding a black bag of some sort. It looks like something a tending doctor may carry with him when visiting patients.

The King asks, "We know the wizard, Droart, is dead. Where is Lord Fulke?"

I watch as there is shifting of legs and arms amongst the Hunters. But none answer. A number of the Hunters protectively fold their arms across their chests. It is a position that Laurence has used many times. I am familiar with it. Their mannerism is one of defense.

They do not trust us.

I turn to the King and say, "My King, I believe the people need a little more information. The ones who have joined us do not know what we know."

He turns to me and says, "Please."

I clear my throat and say, "We know what has happened to your people: the threat Lord Fulke made to you about releasing the deadly Rescol on your newly found city. You must understand we did not know what happened in our village until we came here and learned it was the wizard Droart who brought it on Rumbling Town so many years ago. It claimed the lives of my parents, and as children, Alwyn, Constance, Laurence, and myself watched firsthand as our parents perished from it. They ran a fever for a few days before they could no longer breathe. In the last moments, they gasped together, and with eyes widened, they turned a blue-grey color and held hands. My mother died first, followed swiftly by my father. In a few minutes, we were orphans.

"You must understand, Wyndham and the King knew it was Droart and Lord Fulke who had released Rescol on Rumbling Town. But the only witness died from the illness. They had no evidence, and without such, they could do nothing.

Today, we have more than necessary proof of the plan that was laid and the treachery woven at the hands of Lord Fulke with the help of the wizard on your people. Lord Fulke will be punished for what he has done. The wizard has already paid for his sins with his death, as told to us by Laurence. With the wizard gone, Lord Fulke is only a man."

The man who led the way from the castle, followed by other Hunters, says, "Yes, as already mentioned, the wizard is gone. I know this to be true. He was frozen, thanks to the dragon. I ended him with my sword!" he bellows.

Our King flinches when he hears the man's words. In a calm tone, he says, "The wizard should have been tried, and justice dispensed."

"Justice was dispensed, my King. The wizard fashioned such a terrible illness, I did not want him to walk this world. In truth, we do not know where the mixture for Rescol is; he showed it to us once, and it was in a bottle of some sort. Although, if I had to guess, I would suspect it may be in the black bag the child carries," he says as he points in the direction of Jayden.

I wait only a second. The King says nothing in answer to the man who just spoke.

I continue and say, "Together, we can capture Lord Fulke, too. But we need your help to find him."

One man says, "Hee wus on thee field in ay cloake, last I saw of im."

I begin to scan the assembled group, as my pulse races.

There was a cloaked man …

Somewhere.

My eyes rest on Jayden. Behind her, a few meters away, there is a man. When he catches my eye, he throws off his cloak and races towards the child. There is a piercing high-pitched cry from Constance, who had shifted somewhat away from the child. She runs towards Jayden and steps in front of her. Behind Lord Fulke, a man charges forward, knocking the rogue to the ground. Lord Fulke is facedown in the dirt and lands at the feet of my sister.

Osgoode uses all of his weight to push Lord Fulke

further into the ground. He places a small knife to his throat and spits at him, saying, "Do not move. Or, I will end you here."

***

"My King, you are a foolish ruler!" Lord Fulke screeches at the King. Osgoode pulls him up on his feet, still with the knife resting lightly at his throat.

Constance kneels down to me and says, "Jayden, sweet girl, are you hurt?"

I huff and struggle to breathe. But I don't want to worry, Constance. It begins as a whisper, but I force the word out a little louder near the end and say, "Yeah."

Wyndham arrives and stands beside me. He kneels and says, "Perhaps, it is best that I take the bag from you until I teach you how to use a sword."

"Okay," I say as I swing the bag over to Wyndham by the handle.

Constance clutches my hand tightly and with tears in her eyes, says, "I am not letting you out of my sight. We went so far together. And in the end, I nearly lost you!"

I'm sandwiched between Constance and Wyndham. I whisper, "I'm heavily protected now."

Constance raises one eyebrow, and with her chin raised, she peers down at me and says, "YES!"

Osgoode pushes Lord Fulke forward with the knife at his throat.

The King waves a hand at Lord Fulke and says, "I will show you mercy, Fulke. I will not have you charged with being disrespectful to your King." He pauses and adds, "For we have many charges against you. You will be in prison for the rest of your days. Even if you lived as long as the Great White Dragon, you would never see another sunrise."

"I did it for Canonsland!" Lord Fulke shrieks. He

throws his hands up in the air. The knight, Edric, arrives with another man. They pull Lord Fulke's arms behind his back and clasp them together with chains. No longer needed, Osgoode walks away.

I AM TERRIFIED.

It's probably from Lord Fulke charging at me. But his words, movements, and actions don't make any sense to me. I don't like people like him. People you can't figure out based on what they say, how they say it, or their actions. Most people are road maps. They're sad for a reason, or mad, and you can explain why they feel the way they do.

But there's no explanation for anything Lord Fulke does.

He just hates everyone.

I quietly take a step backward while still holding Constance's hand. She notices the pull and turns to me, and that causes Wyndham to glance in my direction as well. Wyndham steps in front of Constance, and she takes a step backward to be with me. She wraps both her arms around me, holding me tightly, and I lean against her waist. I poke my head out, though. I'm still scared. But I want to see what's going on.

Oh no. It's like watching a scary movie in real life.

Suddenly, there's a cry from the crowd, and a man says, "You killed our people, Lord Fulke! You did not do this for Canonsland!" The man swings his sword out and rushes towards Lord Fulke.

I bury my face in Constance's waist, so I can't see what's happening.

I don't like Lord Fulke, but I can't watch him be killed either!

Then, I hear Laurence's voice. It is raised as he says, "Henry, you cannot do this! Let the laws of Canonsland take care of him. You must trust in that!"

I can't stop myself. I pop my head up. Laurence holds Henry's arm in the air that clutches the sword. Several of the King's guards are also holding Henry back from behind.

There is laughing from Lord Fulke, with a smug smile.

That look. I've seen it before—Lord Fulke glances at Henry as if he's an insect—as if he's worthless—and might as well not even exist.

Lord Fulke says, "No, sir, you did."

"You made us!" Henry screams over Laurence's shoulder while pushing forward. The other guards pull him back. Laurence forcefully takes the sword from Henry.

Lord Fulke continues with his wicked smile; he raises his eyebrows, lowers his chin, and says, "You always had a choice. The blood of your people, are on your hands. Not mine."

The King turns to Lord Fulke, waving at him, and says, "No, Fulke. You gave the order for them to kill their own people by threatening them with Rescol. You have blood on your hands."

The King pauses. There's a quietness that hangs in the air. We're waiting. There's something more the King's going to say. And I suspect we're not going to like it.

The King steps towards Henry and says, "But Fulke is right. There was a choice."

Henry's head is raised; his chin is punched out. His jaw is tight. Tears flood his eyes, but he holds them back.

I can't watch this. There have been too many terrible things that have happened to the Hunters. Why should they be punished?

I search the crowd for Osgoode. I see he's standing next to Enisseny. His head is bowed. He might be quietly crying.

And, he's alone.

Again.

Enisseny wraps his tail around Osgoode, and he pushes him gently with it. Osgoode collapses and sits on Enisseny's foot, with his head still bent forward. Enisseny's eyes are a rich, dark brown now. He turns his head back to me and blinks a couple of times.

The King says, "Your people will live with what they have done for the rest of their days. If, in the future, some terrible choice is presented to the Hunters again, remember this day. Learn from your history. I, too, will remember this day. Canonsland failed your people when we abandoned you two hundred years ago. When faced with such a malicious man as Fulke, and with no friends to help, you would feel the pressure to bend to such a man with the threat of Rescol. In truth, the blood of your people rests heavily on all those who live in Canonsland."

The King spins around to face Henry and says, "And never again, shall this man be spoken of as Lord Fulkc. He is not a Lord. Not here, nor in any land."

The air is heavy. There's a calmness that I can't explain, as if we were in church, and we've heard a sermon that's moved us.

Responsibility. Maybe taking responsibility does that to people.

Henry's eyes stare at the king through tears. But he no longer fights the guards that hold him. He says, "Yes, my King."

The King whirls around to face Fulke. With a dismissive hand raised as if he doesn't matter, the King says, "Take him away."

Two knights and a couple of the soldiers try to pull him away. Fulke fights and says, "What will you do, my

King if another drought sweeps across the land? We can use the dragon, travel to other realms, and take that which we need—food, water!"

There was a lot of space between the King and Fulke. The King's shoulders are forward, his chin has dropped, and he takes giant strides towards the chained man, closing the gap between them.

The King stands inches away from him. In a way that seems appropriate, he also stands above Fulke.

Everyone is on edge. Several of the King's knights rush towards the King. I notice Edric and the other knight hold Fulke tighter. Wyndham does not move. He stands firmly in his place in front of Constance. I'm worried something terrible will happen to the King, and I don't want to see it, but I continue to stare anyway.

"If another great drought sweeps across our land, we will conserve. The same as we did before. However, this time, none of my people will be forgotten!" the King bellows at Fulke as he peers down at him.

We are all focussed on the King, so we don't see it.

A man reaches over the top of Edric's shoulder and jabs a needle into the neck of Fulke.

The King shouts at the man, "What have you done?"

Fulke's body instantly crumples to the ground.

"What?" the man says.

I remember that man. He's the King's doctor.

"I wanted to shut him up. He's scaring Jayden," the doctor says as he smiles and waves in my direction.

"Don't worry," he says, as he faces the frowning King. The doctor waves a careless hand over Fulke. "He's just asleep. Besides, he'll be easier to move now and definitely quieter."

For the first time all day, the King laughs and nods in agreement. He says to the knights, "Take the prisoner away."

The doctor lifts his chin and says, "Alwyn's awake."

CHAPTER 18

I was going to hang back and let Eustace, Constance, Laurence, and Wyndham visit with Alwyn first, but everyone says I'm one of the family now.

Alwyn's SUPER pale. He gently tugs at his blanket, pulling it up to his chin. But he smiles and says, "Did I miss much? What do you need me to do?"

Wyndham stares down at him, places his hand on his shoulder as if he's about to task him with some great quest, and says, "Get well, Alwyn."

"What of Enisseny?" he questions.

With arms folded across his chest, Laurence leans against the wall of the garden cave and says, "Jayden rescued the dragon. Droart is no more. Fulke is captured. Osgoode saved the maiden, and Jayden. You have slept through the best parts of the story, brother."

"Oh, well. Perhaps it is for the best. I fear I am not very good with a sword. Perhaps, I should go home and tend to things there."

"I agree," Laurence says. "But if you do need protection, Constance is better than you, and she can defend you if she must."

168

"What is this?" Alwyn's eyebrows come together, as he pulls himself up to more of a sitting position.

Eustace says, "Wyndham has taught Constance how to use a sword. He has instructed her for years in secrecy."

"Well, that explains why I am not good, because you did not commit the same time to teach me, as you did to my sister." Alwyn looks sideways at Wyndham with a grin.

"No, I did. But you and Eustace never took to it the way Laurence and Constance did," Wyndham says.

"Well," Alwyn glances at Eustace and says, "Eustace is too busy talking."

Eustace laughs. "'Tis true. I am still here, thanks to Gamel. I fear I am not very good in battle, either."

"Gamel? Who is he?"

"'Tis one of the guards that Eustace and Constance held here in the Garden Cave, as Jayden calls it," Laurence says while facing me. "You have truly missed much, dear brother. Gamel, joined us, in the end."

"Someday, someone must recount the tale to me. But while I have some strength, I wish to say some things." Alwyn's voice breaks apart when he says this.

"No more serious conversation on this day. We have had quite a bit of it from the King. Poor Jayden has had a dreadful first visit with us. She will never come again," Wyndham says. He gazes down at me with a mixed smile I can't read.

Does Wyndham think I won't come back? I mean, it hasn't been as much fun as I thought it would be. I've been terrified a lot of the time. I've seen and heard people do terrible things. But a lot of people have really taken care of me. Now that I remember back, climbing the rock wall was cool—even if Laurence dropped me. Twice. I rub my forehead, and my hand sweeps over a massive bump there.

Man, it's a good thing I fell down and bumped my head on the dresser. That will be an explanation, at least, when Mom sees the lump. Everything's back together here, sort of. With that thought, an overwhelming sense of relief sweeps across me, and I let out a big sigh.

I'll have to go home soon and talk to Mom and Dad. I'm going to tell them everything I know. Just like Constance told me to do.

"You should definitely come back," the doctor says. "There are lots of things to see." He shrugs his shoulders and adds, "Maybe you'll decide to move here, too."

I shout, "I can't believe I didn't notice! We talk the same."

"Yup," he says. "Much more direct. Less 'tis's." We both laugh at the joke, and so does everyone else.

"I would come back," I say before I can stop myself. I begin to twirl my fingertips together and quickly add, "If I were invited."

"Always," Wyndham says.

"Excuse me. Anyone remember me? I am the man who took a sword in battle and was stitched up? I need to say some things," as Alwyn says these words, his eyes are shifting back and forth to everyone. He looks frustrated and emotional. He pulls himself up a little more on his cot as if he wants to make sure we don't forget about him again.

"Please," Wyndham says.

We all hush, and the doctor quietly leaves to take care of other people who are injured from both sides of the battle.

"Laurence, I wish to tell you ... I believe you will make a great knight. But if ever the need should arise, I will always find you and help you. You are my brother."

Laurence moves from foot to foot and doesn't say anything right away. Then he sticks his chin out, peers down at Alwyn, and whispers, "You do not need to."

Alwyn moves a leg. I see a blood vessel on his forehead pop up. He says, "I know I do not need to. But you will always be my brother. Even as a knight."

"'Tis good," Wyndham says, facing Laurence. "I have you as my children, and now as my siblings. But I had brothers, long ago. I miss them."

It's the first time on my visit that Wyndham has ever talked about his other family. He's smiling, but there's pain there, too. Something he mentioned about Rumbling Town comes back to me: He told me the people of Rumbling Town never wanted to live forever because you would be the last one left.

Wyndham's smiling, but I know he's faking it, just like Mom does.

"I will need to be more careful then," Laurence says. "My brothers do not do well with swords. But, if my sister comes, I will have no need to worry." He grins sheepishly at Constance.

"Perhaps, Constance should become a knight, too?" Eustace poses the question we're all thinking.

"There are women who are knights," Wyndham announces with a nod of his head. His eyes stare at Constance as he waits for an answer.

We're all waiting.

"I know, Father. But I do not wish to be one," Constance says with a firm smile. "'Tis not the path for me, and I know that. But I can protect those I care for. I am not helpless. For that, Father, I thank you."

Wyndham's eyebrows scrunch together. He asks, "Why have you begun calling me 'Father' again?"

"Because," Constance says, "you cared for us, fed us,

171

and clothed us, and worked hard to make sure as children that we felt safe and loved. You are our father. I know we had other parents, and they were good parents. But you took us when no one else would and never considered separating us. I am certain you had moments when you thought it would have been better to do so …."

Constance blushes and smiles while she waits for all of us to stop laughing at her joke.

"You did not. I wish to call you 'Father,' if you permit me, for the rest of my days."

Oh, no. I think Wyndham might cry. And if he cries, I might cry.

"My sister has stolen my words. That is what I wished to say," Alwyn says with a smile. "Jayden, do you have siblings?" he asks as he glances over at me.

I shake my head, no.

"This is what is called sibling rivalry," he says, with a small snap in his voice at the end of it. "They steal your words, leaving you with nothing to say, even though you've had a great amount of time to think about and reword it a thousand times in your mind. Then, your sister comes in and says it better than you, without preparing for the speech!"

Everyone laughs in the room.

Wyndham says, "You will grow old, and I do not age the same, as everyone else. At some point, it may seem odd to you. And I do not wish to replace your parents." Wyndham's words tumble out of him like dominos falling. Wyndham laughed at Alwyn's joke. But he shifts uncomfortably from one foot to the other as he waits for a response.

"It will not bother me if I live for one hundred years, and I call you 'Father,' even if you never change," Eustace says. "And I know my siblings agree."

Wyndham's chin is pulled down, and he nods his head. He won't look at anyone. He huffs, and before he can say anything, we hear from behind us, "I do not wish to interrupt ..."

"Please, come in, Osgoode," Wyndham says with relief, as he glances up at the voice. "My children, they are making me uncomfortable."

Constance grins, her face lights up, and she says, "Yes, the steely knight is unable to speak about his emotions."

Her eyes sweep from Wyndham to Osgoode. When they land on Osgoode, her features change instantly: Her brows furrow together, and her lips straighten. "What is it that you carry?" she asks in a quiet voice.

"It is a few things," Osgoode says. He places a bag against the side of the wall and folds his hands together in front of him.

"I wish to give my thanks for all that you have done and the sacrifices you have made for our people. I do not know if the other Hunters would say so ..." Osgoode's voice wobbles on the last word. The word "so" dangles in midair. It's as if he's misplaced the other part of the sentence that would come after that. Just like the other part of that sentence that's lost, Osgoode's eyes spin around the room. He won't make eye contact with anyone directly. Not even Constance. He's quite a distance away from us. For a big, big guy—he seems so small.

Constance crosses the floor. She places a hand on his arm. "What is in the satchel? Are you leaving?" she asks.

"I cannot stay here, Constance. My parents, brother, sisters, all of them have been killed—even Toly. If Toly would have lived, I may have forgiven him, as he saved my life. We were friends and were like brothers. But he is gone, too."

Osgoode raises a hand and rubs his eye. It's shaking. He pulls it down and places his other hand against it to stop it. He says, "I understand why they did it. I can forgive. But I cannot forget. Not yet. I need to go away."

"Where will you go?" Constance whispers to him.

"I do not know," he says. "My people wandered this world for hundreds of years. I can find food along the way ... perhaps, work in the odd village or town if they will have me, and thus earn my keep there."

"I would have you," Constance answers without hesitating.

Osgoode smiles at her. "Maybe in time, if I can make a home for us. I would like that. But I cannot do it now. I have nothing."

"I would have you, too!" Alwyn chimes in. "There is a lot of work to do in our decrepit castle and on the land. I have two knights who wander off endlessly: one on official knightly duties, and the other, to do whatever he likes. I have another one here ..." Alwyn waves a hand at Eustace and says, "This one spends too much time thinking and talking."

We all stare at Osgoode for a few moments. "I do not know what to say," Osgoode answers. "Your family has done a great deal for me. I cannot ask for more."

Wyndham says, "Do not ask Osgoode to make a decision in front of everyone. Let him consider it. But I must say something as well. It may help you, Osgoode, to come to a resolution ... Young Laurence will be spending more time with me now that I know he does not do his chores." Wyndham's arms are folded in front of him as he stands in front of Laurence now and says, "You will see, Laurence, there is more to being a knight than swordsmanship. But, now, Alwyn will be short one more person."

"It will be two, Father," Eustace says to Wyndham. He pauses and then adds, "The King believes I may be suited to a life of diplomacy. And as such, he has offered me a position. I did not want to leave straight away. I wanted to spend time with Alwyn and ensure the old man is on the mend. I, however, cannot put it off forever. Thus, Alwyn will be down two men."

"Finally! All those years of being the diplomat in our family, and you have found your path." Alwyn smiles at Eustace. There's a glow in his eyes. He might be making fun of him, but the way Alwyn perked up when Eustace told us about his new position, I know he's proud of him, too.

"You must come," Alwyn demands as he faces Osgoode.

***

Me, Bob, Wyndham, and Alwyn flew on Enisseny back to Rumbling Town. It was beautiful. Enisseny soared so high, and this time his wings were so quiet all I heard was the whistling of the wind. When we passed over a town, there were small dots below us of homes and people that walked along roads. Every now and then, Enisseny would swoop down closer so that I could see the village, trees, flowers, and people better. Children who saw us waved to us, and Wyndham encouraged me to wave back to them.

Alwyn was holding Bob in a cloth sack, and they both freaked out together. I don't think Alwyn likes flying. He moaned and groaned the whole way, and he really didn't like the swooping. Then again, Alwyn nearly fell off, so that probably didn't help. I was the one who reached across and grabbed his arm to keep him upright; I also grabbed the bag that Bob was in that Alwyn carried.

If Bob didn't like flying before, he sure doesn't like it

now.

When we land, Alwyn's sick. He says it's his wound. Panicking, I glance up at Wyndham. Wyndham shakes his head from side to side and whispers to me, "He has never enjoyed soaring through the clouds on Enisseny. As a child, he would become ill, too."

Then Wyndham walks over to him, helps him up, and as Alwyn leans on him, Wyndham says, "I'm certain 'tis the reason."

Idonea and Petronilla come running out of the castle. Idonea is carrying something in her hands that she drops when she sees Alwyn, and it makes a *cracking* sound when it hits the ground. Idonea's legs fly underneath her and Petronilla's face turns the color of snow, as she runs behind her mother. Idonea screams, "Alwyn!" It sends shivers down my spine because it reminds me of Constance when she first saw Alwyn after he had been stabbed with a sword.

Wyndham raises his one free hand and shouts, "Alwyn will be fine! But, he requires some rest."

Idonea stands in front of Alwyn, and her lower lip goes up and down. With her hands shaking in front of her, Idonea says, "Alwyn?"

"I am alright, my love," he says with tears in his eyes. They wrap their arms around each other. Petronilla arrives now, and their eyes are all red-rimmed as they hold each other for what feels like forever.

Wyndham and I stand back, look at each other, and smile.

"What was it that you dropped?" Alwyn finally asks.

"Was gondeling pie," Idonea says, laughing. Alwyn leans on her. Idonea holds him up as they slowly walk back to the castle.

"'Tis, too bad. I love your gondeling pie."

"Tomorrow, I will make another for you, my love," she says with a quiet laugh as she leans against his chest.

Laurence, Eustace, and Constance are all riding horses back to town. Osgoode has agreed to follow them here as there is nowhere specific he has to be anyway.

Wyndham asks, "What thoughts wander the mind of Jayden that keeps you so quiet?"

"I'm worried about Osgoode. So much has happened to him. Will he be alright?" I ask with hesitation in my voice.

He says, "I do, indeed hope so. Do not underestimate my children. They knew Enisseny could carry all of us back to Rumbling Town. Eustace, Constance, and Laurence chose to travel by horse to convince Osgoode to stay with us. That is their task, one I hope ends happily. Perhaps, even with a marriage between Constance and Osgoode."

I glimpse up at Wyndham and ask, "Do they love each other?"

Wyndham says, "Love takes time to grow between two people. But, yes, they have laid the soil for it to blossom. It may indeed become love."

Wyndham stops when we approach the door of the castle. He says, "Jayden, I will see if Idonea might run you a bath. We will find the clothes you wore when you arrived, and give you some food. But you must move quickly. You must return to your room in the next few hours; otherwise, your parents will believe you to be missing. We do not wish to worry them more, as they now face new obstacles."

I breathe out hard and say, "I understand. I'll hurry." I grab the door handle and push it open and begin to run.

"Jayden, what will you do?" Wyndham asks.

I'm halfway up the stairs, stop, and spin around to

answer Wyndham's question. I'm remembering everything I saw and did. It moves through my mind in slow motion. Sometimes it's as if I have a pause button in my brain, and I will stop it on some things like when I was flying in Enisseny's palm. It was frightening at the time, but now I realize it was also AMAZING! We traveled so fast, causing the wind to blow my hair around everywhere, and the view of Canonsland was beautiful. When Enisseny closed his talons, it was warm inside, and the rocking motion of the flight eventually helped me sleep.

Other parts, I fast-forward through, like watching Osgoode cry multiple times because he's lost everyone he loved.

I hated that.

But I'm not as scared of stuff, as I was when I first arrived in Canonsland. I smile a little at meeting the Dragon and Wyndham (finally!), climbing up the rock with no plan to save Laurence from Osgoode, releasing Enisseny from his chains, and meeting many new friends.

I scrunch my face up. Looking down at Wyndham from the stairs—which never happens!—I answer, "I'm going to talk to Mom and Dad. Tell them what I know. I'll be okay if I stay with my grandparents for a few months if Mom needs me to. If it means she'll get better."

Wyndham proudly smiles at me, just like Alwyn did at Eustace when Eustace told us about his new job with the King.

Finally, Wyndham says, "Enisseny and I, we will see you when you return."

I spin around and begin to run again, with Bob wobbling beside me. He really didn't like the flight. Then I stop. I remember my manners and say, "Thank you for inviting me for a visit. It was nice to finally meet you and Enisseny, for real."

"No, it is I who should thank you. You saved my dragon." Wyndham pauses and says with a smile, "Just as with Osgoode, Enisseny knows a person's heart. He knew you needed us long ago, and also at this time in your life. But he knew we needed you, as well."

For the first time in my life, I feel like I matter.

"Jayden, move with haste!" Wyndham's eyebrows pop up, as he begins chuckling. His face and his words snap me back to where I am and what I have to do.

"Oh, right!" I shout as I run, taking the stairs two at a time.

CHAPTER 19

I open my eyes. Based on what Wyndham said, this should be the next day, even though I spent a couple of weeks in Canonsland. Wyndham said time moves faster there. I can't be gone for long stretches of times without being missed at home, but shorter timeframes are possible without anyone noticing. As long as Mom and Dad didn't check on me in the middle of the night, they'd have no idea I was gone.

I move my right foot to get out of bed, and I kick a soft, furry, cuddly thing that's in the way. Staring back at me with big pleading eyes—as if to ask *what did you do that for?*—is an adorable mass of cuteness that I love so much.

Bob, unwilling to wait any longer, walks down to where my head is and begins to lick my face.

I giggle quietly and push him back gently. I whisper, "Bob, you know you're not allowed on my bed."

As if he understands every word I've said, he drops his head to the bed and lies flat-faced against my mattress. Pouty puppy has arrived. He's trying to get his own way.

"Well …." I pause for a moment and peer down at him. "If you don't tell Mom and Dad about Canonsland,

I won't tell them you slept on the bed. Deal?" I ask.

Bob's head instantly bounces up, and he uses the opportunity to drench me in more slobber as his tongue sweeps across my face. I take his kibble-breath kisses to mean we have an agreement.

My nose is inches away from Bob. He has bad breath, but his coat smells like berries! Wyndham bathed him before we left with goldenberries that grow on the fields of Wyndham's family's Castle.

I wonder if Bob may smell too good. I consider spraying Bob with some of Mom's perfume. It may hide the smell of the goldenberries. If Mom and Dad ask, I can tell them Bob smelled terrible, so I sprayed some of Mom's perfume on him until we have a chance to bathe him.

No, I decide. There are too many other important things to worry about. They probably won't notice. If they do, I'll just play dumb. Or, I'll say I thought they bathed Bob while I was at school.

I wiggle away from Bob, push back my covers, and walk over to the mirror. There's no one there—just me and my reflection with a GIGANTIC bump on my forehead. I pull my bangs over the lump. You can still see it. Then I attempt to push all my hair to the side. I could tell Mom I'm trying a new hairstyle. But I need to pull ALL of my hair to one side, and the goose egg still shows. Also, "the new hairstyle" makes me look ridiculous. Frustrated, I huff and mumble, "Laurence, did you have to let go of the rope … twice?"

Behind me, I hear the sound of muffled snorting that comes from my bed. I spin around, and Bob's rubbing his face into my sheets. He's upside-down with his feet sticking into the air. With both eyes open, Bob stares blankly past me for a moment and then starts to roll to the right and then left on his back, with jowls hanging down. He must be happy to be home—and glad to sleep in my bed!

But we've got work to do. I dress in a few seconds, pulling on blue jeans, a grey T-shirt, and socks. I say, "Come on, Bob." Then I pull my bangs down as far as they will go and walk to the bedroom door, placing my hand on the doorknob.

Bob is frozen on my bed. Not a paw moves, or a leg, or even so much as a whisker.

"Come on, Bob," I whisper. "I'm tired, too, but we have to talk to Mom and Dad."

Bob rolls over and faces the wall, turning his back on me. I breathe out in annoyance. I'm not mad that Bob's not coming; I just wish I could stay in bed, too, and more importantly, not have this conversation with my parents.

Bob's been with me through everything in Canonsland. When he wasn't with me, he took care of Alwyn. Alwyn said he never left his side the whole time, and the doctor told me he had to convince Bob to get off the bed to eat his meals.

"Fine," I say, "you can sit this one out. I'll talk to Mom and Dad."

I pull the door to my room closed, and behind it, I hear a deep snore. Bob, most likely, is already fast asleep.

***

I enter the kitchen. Mom leaps to attention.

"Where's Dad?" I ask in a quiet voice.

She says, "Oh, he's fixing the roof, honey." It's an answer to my question, but she's pulled the fridge door open and continues with, "Can I make you something? Eggs? Maybe, French toast?" Her whole head is in the fridge. The sound of bottles sliding around in the fridge continues for a few seconds until one of the jars falls over with a *clunk!* It doesn't sound as if it broke, only that it fell over. Mom continues to push things around and says, "Uhmmm … I think I have bacon in here?"

Mom, with her head hiding in the fridge, is how I leave her. I swing the front door open and then push the screen door open as well. I'm not paying attention, and I hear both doors vibrate when they bounce closed. I hear some words, and they sound faintly like, "Jayden?"

I climb a ladder that's leaning against our house. When I get to the top of it, I poke my head over the roof, and I see Dad.

I announce, "Dad, we need to talk."

Dad nearly slips off the roof when he sees me. I leap from the ladder to the roof to grab him because I can't lose my dad.

I need both parents.

"Jayden, what are you doing up here?" he asks. "You're terrified of heights. Please, get down!" he shouts the last part at me.

"Dad, don't fall," I say quietly. I slide backward and place my feet back on the ladder. I'm not afraid, but he's panicking on my behalf, so he's not paying attention. He's going to hurt himself.

"Oh, and I'm not afraid of heights anymore," I announce. My thoughts are becoming a jumbled mess, and I know if I wait too long, I'll lose my nerve and not have the conversation that I need to have with them. I ask, "Could you come down? I need to talk to you and Mom."

As I steer backward down the ladder, with each foot bouncing on each step, I notice that Mom's shaking hands are holding it. Dad walks on the roof, and a few seconds later, he follows me.

When I get to the bottom and jump on the grass,

Mom shouts, "I don't want you on ladders! You could get hurt!" She pauses for a moment, and then says, "Oh, god, what happened to your head?" Her hands continue to shake, and now she has tears in her eyes.

"I got hurt," I say in a calm voice.

Mom gives me a look as if I've stung her. She steps back from me. Dad is there, too, now, and he heard what I said. My face flushes. Silence has swept in and strangled the air between us.

I have to smooth this out. My answer to Mom's question is the truth. But it needs more explanation. I'm channeling Eustace here and his ability to talk, and so I need to give more details about the lump on my forehead.

But it can't be the whole truth.

I say, "Remember when I tripped on my pants last night? I hit my head on the dresser. I told you and Dad about that."

Mom smiles and touches my forehead to take a closer look, and says, "Right. I forgot. But, Robert, look at this?"

Dad's hands are covered in black dirt, and he rubs my forehead with them and says, "Yeah, that looks pretty bad. "

Mom's shaking more now and says, "I should take her to the doctor. Get some X-rays just to make sure she's alright."

I now know how Alwyn felt when we came to visit him, and he tried to share his feelings with his family and couldn't get it out because other family members kept hijacking his conversation. It's as if you're all out riding together, and several of them gallop off in different directions, and you're stuck in the middle, trying to figure out who you should follow because you're the only one who knows there's a forest fire closing in on everyone.

But no one would listen to you for the two seconds when you were all in the same place.

It's frustrating.

I back away from my parents. Raising my hands to both of them, I hold my palms out and motion for them stop. I say, "Mom, if you want to take me for X-rays, I'll go. I don't want to make things difficult for you. I know you're sick."

Mom covers her mouth. Her eyes fill with tears as she says, "How do you know?"

I stare at the ground and start kicking the dirt. All these years, and I've never told them how much I know—or, how I know it. *Time to tell.*

I flick my eyes back and forth between Mom and Dad. I mumble, "I'm awake some nights when you and Dad go to bed. I hear you guys talking."

Small quiet streams of water drip from the corners of mom's eyes. She folds one arm protectively across her chest and places her other hand to her lips and mumbles, "Do you know what's wrong?"

I should lie to her. But I don't. My eyebrows pull together, my lips pucker out as they already have so many times before when I was alone, and I whisper, "Cancer."

The dam bursts. Tears flow down my cheeks like a waterfall.

Mom wraps her arms around me in one of her bear hugs, and we stay like that for a few moments. Dad stands back. Then, he places one hand on both our necks, and we both grab him and pull him in.

Finally, as a family no longer separated, we cry together.

Then, we all take a deep breath.

***

One month later, after school is out for me, we're all

standing at the airport. Mom and Dad have helped me check my bags in and get my boarding pass, and now I'm about to go through security.

The first day I returned from Canonsland, we talked and talked until there was nothing left to say. I told Mom and Dad, I thought they were sending me away because I made things difficult for them. Mom and Dad said that wasn't the reason—they were sending me away because they couldn't give me a happy childhood because money was always tight, and if I had to watch my mom go through cancer treatment, that would ruin what's left of it.

We're not very good at communicating. Me and Mom both blamed Dad. (As a joke).

I told them I knew we were poor, but I had really *amazing* parents, and so I didn't need a lot of stuff. Just like that, I said it.

I didn't tell them everything, though. I didn't say I was afraid something would happen to Mom during treatment and that I was worried she might leave us. But I kind of hinted about it when I asked if I could come home if I was worried about her and needed to see her. They agreed I could.

When I talked to Grandpa about it on the phone, I told him I knew they didn't have a lot of money, and it would be hard for them to send me back home if I wanted to get back quickly. Grandpa said, *Jayden, I'll drive you back myself if I have to. And if you really need to be home, we'll find the money for the airfare. Don't you worry about that— me and Grandma, we'll figure something out.*

At the end of the conversation with my parents on that day, I agreed to stay with Grandma and Grandpa for the summer. I told my parents I knew it was important for Mom to take care of herself because she needed to focus on getting better.

Mom started to cry.

And Dad almost did, too!

Dad's eyes fill up with tears at the security gate. He says, "Are you sure you're okay to fly by yourself?" Before I can answer, he says, "I really wish you hadn't told Grandpa he didn't have to come and fly with you."

Mom and Dad don't know that I flew on Enisseny. They have no idea. "Dad, I'll be fine," I say with a wave of my hand. "Stop worrying."

Dad's eyes are glossy. He says, "I'll always worry about you, Jayden."

I remember the conversation between Alwyn and Laurence. Alwyn used different words, but the meaning was the same. I say to Dad, "I know."

"Sorry?" Mom stares hard at Dad and says with a little sparkle in her eye, "Are we having a forbidden *squishy* moment?" Her hands are on her hips, and she's started to tap her foot.

Me and Mom bend forward in laughter. Dad turns his head away from us for a second and raises a finger to the corner of his eye like Gamel did. When he faces us again, his cheeks are pink; he smiles and says, "What do you expect? I live in a house filled with women."

"Okay. Well, Mom, this is your assignment—" I say seriously. I stick a finger out, pointing at Dad and say, "You need to beat that out of him while I'm gone."

Mom laughs and laughs and finally says, "I shall make it my utmost priority, Daughter."

I roll my eyes.

I don't know why—but ever since we talked that day—even though I never told my parents about Canonsland—Mom tries to talk like Wyndham and the other people there.

My parents don't know about Wyndham going missing, Enisseny's rescue, or all the terrible stuff that happened to the Hunters. In this place, it's my secret.

And Bob's.

I kiss them both, and we all hug. Dad says, "Okay, and Uncle John will bring Bob up in a couple of weeks."

"Thanks, Dad," I say. It was a requirement. Bob had to come, too.

I start to go through the security gates, and I turn and wave to them one final time. I carry a knapsack that has a few things in it to do during the flight. One of the things I brought was a book on grizzly bears and what to do if you encounter one. Grandpa suggested it.

I stop.

Just before I go through security, I twirl around and face my parents one more time. I drop my knapsack on the ground.

Mom and Dad step forward as a puzzled, concerned expression stretches across their faces.

From a distance, I curtsy to them and say, "My Lord, My Lady, 'til we meet again."

Mom throws her hands over her mouth. Dad places a hand casually on her neck and pulls her close to him. Mom buries her face in his chest, but one eye stays on me.

My parents laugh at their daughter.

The daughter who lives in two worlds: here and Canonsland.

ABOUT THE AUTHOR

Penelope S. Hawtrey lives in Northeastern Canada with her husband, "attack" chocolate Labrador, and her "secret" bug collection. Growing up in Southern Ontario, she learned the value of hard work from her parents, and post-graduation from University, she held numerous administrative roles in various industries.

In 2016, Penelope published several short stories on Amazon. From one of the short stories initially released, she worked to create her first full-length novel, *Dragon in the Mirror: Into Canonsland.* This is the first book in a planned series.

For all the latest updates on Penelope, including upcoming projects, release dates, and scheduled appearances check out her website at www.penelopeshawtrey.com or follow her on Twitter @pshawtrey.

Made in the USA
Middletown, DE
19 January 2020